Cleavage)(

Theanna Bischoff

NeWest Press

copyright © Theanna Bischoff 2008

Library and Archives Canada Cataloguing in Publication

Bischoff, Theanna, 1984-
Cleavage / Theanna Bischoff.

(Nunatak fiction)
ISBN 978-1-897126-25-7

I. Title. II. Series.

PS8603.I83C54 2008   C813'.6   C2007-906071-4

Editor for the Board: Suzette Mayr
Cover and interior design: Natalie Olsen
Cover image: Natalie Olsen
Author photo: Alyssa Adair

NeWest Press acknowledges the support of the Canada Council for the Arts, the Alberta Foundation for the Arts, and the Edmonton Arts Council for our publishing program. We also acknowledge the financial support of the Government of Canada through the Book Publishing Industry Development Program (BPIDP).

NeWest Press
#201 8540.109 Street
Edmonton, Alberta T6G 1E6
780.432.9427
newestpress.com

No bison were harmed in the making of this book.
We are committed to protecting the environment and to the responsible use of natural resources. This book is printed on 100% recycled, ancient forest-friendly paper.

1 2 3 4 5 11 10 09 08   printed and bound in Canada

For Shannon Teryll Adair,
for being contagious.

)(one

This is how we celebrate our last Valentine's Day together: I draw a heart in spermicide on my diaphragm. The gel forms a protective seal that keeps him away. Inside my body it joins the conference of chemicals, circulates, makes friends. *I'm here to keep her from getting pregnant*, it boasts. To which the chemotherapy laughs, *I don't think you need to worry.*

✂

Hers is the same voice that says, "Your immunoglobulins came back normal," that says, "Your lungs sound healthy," that asks, "Are you taking a multivitamin?" that informs me, "You have a nice cervix." I wonder what it would be like to have a mean cervix.

Hers is the same voice that says, "At twenty-four, your chances of having breast cancer are very, very slim," that says, "Having lumpy breasts is normal," that says, "If you were in your forties … in your thirties, even, I'd do a biopsy. But we might just want to sit on this one for awhile. Wait and see."

✂

Justin's stopping—starting keeps me from sleeping. He cranes his neck to see around a semi, fluid dribbling from its exhaust pipe. I change the radio station.

"When are the dedications? I thought… are we out of range?"

"You missed them. You were sleeping."

"I was never sleeping."

✂

This is how my father reacts to me introducing them: by asking Justin for haggis. "I've always wanted to try it. My ex-wife, uh, Leah's mother, would never … well, you know. She just wasn't very … "

I interrupt, "I think it looks like something that came out of a seasick cat."

My father says, "Why would there be a seasick cat?"

This is how they bond. Just them. Old dad, new boyfriend, Scottish cuisine.

><

In Invermere, the gas station rejects the credit card for our joint account. "It's probably just a mix-up at the bank," Justin says. "You should call them."

I say, "*I* should call them?"

He uses his private card, from a separate bank, which swipes successfully. He buys the melt-in-your-mouth soft Cheetos, beef jerky, an eight-pack of Kotex, $20.03 worth of gas. "You can just pay me back," he says.

I say, "*I can just pay you back?*"

><

His is the same voice that says, "I haven't had a *real* girlfriend, ever," that asks, "Can I kiss you?" that imitates Oscar the Grouch when he's pissed me off, that recites quasi-sexual haikus on our eleven-month anniversary. "Tell your friends your boyfriend writes you poetry."

His is the same voice that says, "You think you feel what? Come here. They feel fine to me. Perfect. As usual. Maybe even bigger."

><

There is no such thing as not knowing. I knew from the moment I dropped the insert from the box of tampons, before I unfolded it, before I stared at the cartoon women holding their arms above their heads, squeezing their nipples, moving their fingers in larger and larger concentric circles. Looking for what I knew was there.

><

Hers is the same voice that asks, "It hasn't moved?"

"It hasn't moved."

I think of my mother, saying that having a mammogram is like running breast-first into a brick wall. When she was in high school gym class, the boys wrestled and the girls placed their palms together, chanting, "We must, we must, we must increase our busts." When I was in high school, the girls took self-defense, jamming our fingers, knees, and fists into the most vulnerable places on a man's body: eyes, nose, throat, groin.

Penticton Itinerary

DAY 1

9:00 AM	Leave Calgary
1:00 PM	Stop in Golden for lunch
6:00 PM	Arrive at Penticton Inn & Suites
	(Check-in after 6:00 PM)
	Standard Superior Room $119 CAD/night
	(Standard Superior???)

DAY 2

10:00 AM	Breakfast
	Hit the beach!!!
12:00 PM	Lunch
1:00 PM	??? More beach ???

When I ask whether Justin wants to learn how to snorkel, he says, "Stop making lists." This is our first vacation as a couple, but it is more than that. This is my first vacation since ending treatment. Does this make me normal? Lovers on vacation, photos behind beetle-eyed sunglasses, the bum of your bathing suit a heart of wet sand? A car without a CD player, a road trip mixed tape, a deliciously expensive but not too expensive splurge on accommodations (an inn! Not quite a hotel, but certainly not a motel). Car games invented during childhood, illicit (!) away-from-home sex, hours of deliberate nothingness.

Do normal people zip tamoxifen bottles into the section of their suitcase where naughty underwear and one very over-priced bikini should be?

✄

His is the same voice that vows, "There's always a second opinion!" that insists, "You're going to beat this thing, pound it into a pulp," that breathes in/out while picturing Terry Fox and his 80s shorts limp around, "Visualize, visualize, Leah," that asks how short my hair will actually get, "Like, *lesbian* short?"

✕

As children, we fought to find the dimes our grandmother baked into our birthday cakes. The bigger the piece, the more likely to find the dime. Sometimes, afterwards, my stomach would hurt, heavy with angel food. I say, take the whole breast.

✕

Justin and my dad debate my treatment options over haggis. Justin tells me this retrospectively; after all, I am not privy to meals of cat regurgitation or debates over the healing possibilities of tree bark. He comes home with brochures about positive thinking, says he thinks I should go back to work as soon as possible, after. My feet are cold. "Can't they, you know, give you that ... you know, what is that treatment? Bone?..."

"That's for leukemia," I tell him. "Cancer of the blood."

"Bone *marrow*!" he gloats. "It was on the tip of my tongue. Thank God, that would have been bugging me all night."

✕

The second night in Penticton, Justin finds a ladybug in his salad, laughs, flicks it off his fingertips, watches it scuttle on the porch balcony. Eats a cherry tomato, "Want one?"

"Want one?"

"Yeah. They're good."

"There was a *bug* in your *salad*."

"And?"

"And?" I think of trapping ladybugs under jars as a child, watching their yellow trails as they scurried along the glass. "What if it ... secreted ... in there?"

"What?"

"You know, in self-defense. They squirt yellow stuff."

"Wetting their pants? Great self-defense." He watches the ladybug trip on a trellis, roll helplessly onto its back. "Face the fear," he tells it.

I think of vomiting in self-defense.

✕

Our two-year anniversary falls during the last two weeks that I have two breasts. Justin finds his old clarinet and plays the opening notes to a vaguely familiar song, so sweet and gentle that I cry. He says, "Thank God for high school band."

We eat soft Cheetos under the kitchen table, using sheets as the walls to his makeshift fort. He eats with his left hand and keeps his right on my sacrificial breast. "I'm Cheeto ambidextrous."

✂

There are things I want these voices to know.

I hate, but will never neglect, shaving my legs and/or taking out the garbage. I own only one piece of real jewellery, a yellow gold anklet, but have worn it everywhere, even once while watching Justin's niece at a petting zoo. I cut kiwis vertically instead of horizontally. I don't have a favourite band, even though everybody asks me that question. I was the smartest kid in the second grade — after that, I just regressed towards the mean. I have never broken a bone, been stung or bitten by an insect of any kind, and I didn't know until last year that pickles were just cucumbers that had marinated in dilly vinegar. I drink root beer Slurpees, even in the winter. I have never once been on an airplane. My mother never once painted my toenails.

The voices prod and cup and adjust. They outline in purple marker; it bleeds into my skin. Connect the dotted line.

✂

Our waitress' skirt is so short, you can see the nude-coloured birth control patch applied firmly to her upper thigh, so upper it is almost bum.

I scratch my signature onto the VISA receipt.

"How much are you tipping her?" Justin asks, then swallows.

"How much am I tipping her?"

"Yeah, you know. It was a pretty big bill. You gotta tip proportional."

"I know it was a big bill. I'm paying for it."

"I'm just curious."

"Be curious in your head."

"We live together, we're on vacation together, but you feel like you have to be secretive?"

"I'm being selective. There's a difference. You don't ask someone how much they're tipping; it's like … it's like asking someone how much your birthday gift cost. It's rude."

"Don't tell me I'm being rude. Let me pay the goddamned bill if you're going to be so uptight about money."

"I'm not —"

✂

It was a delayed response. I went home and showered first. Justin sat, not speaking, on the living room futon and watched stand-up comedy on television. I showered. I staggered out of the shower and began to heave, sank to my knees.

He held my hair back. I thought, *Pretty soon you'll be out of a job: there won't be any hair left to hold up.* "No crying," he said, "Okay? Okay? No crying."

I, on the other hand, thought I was heaving.

His was the voice that said, "Repeat after me, okay? You can't cry if you're saying something funny. Platypus. Come on, Leah, platypus."

I leaned back, shook. My whole body was hot. He was behind me, forcing a towel around me. "Shhh. You're okay. Come on, you can do it. Platypus. Uh … crusty. Um, goblin. Machupichu."

On TV, the comic was still talking.

"So, I'm making out with this hot Asian chick, and she says everybody needs a Chinese name. And I, I look down, and, and … and I say, how about Gung Ho?"

✂

We spread our towels out on Okanagan Beach. They rise and fall with the ripples and mounds of sand beneath. This is the only vacation we've been on in the almost three years we've been together.

I put on sunscreen, SPF 50, lotion and sand rubbed gritty into my skin. I sunscreen the cracks between my fingers, the arches of my feet. I sunscreen any skin visible to the sun, even the line on my scalp, a smear that divides my hair into pigtails, beautifully symmetrical.

"Overkill?" Justin suggests.

ADVANCE DIRECTIVE AND LIVING WILL

I, Leah Isabelle Jordan, being of sound mind, make this statement as a directive to be followed should I become permanently unable to participate in decisions regarding my medical care. These instructions reflect my firm and settled commitment to **pursue** all medical treatment under the circumstances indicated below. The following instructions apply if I am: a) considered terminal; b) rendered permanently unconscious; or c) have irreversible and/or vegetative brain damage.

I do want cardiac resuscitation.

I do want mechanical respiration.

I do want tube feeding.

I do want antibiotics.

I do want maximum pain relief.

I do not want to die.

There was a before.

One time, we (he?) thought it would be funny to drive through McDonalds (Wendy's?) and see whether they would let us have free packages of ketchup (all condiments?). He liked to mix his diet sodas together.

This was like, our third (fourth?) date.

We played a modified game of twenty questions, in which he was the host.

Bad habits? Forgetting to return things, namely, library books.

Aversions? Cigarette smoke, artichokes, couples who pee in front of each other.

Fears? "Rejection," I said, "Failure. Death. Abandonment."

"No," he said, "Those are everybody's fears. What are *your* fears?"

"Um," I said, "I'm scared of losing things. You know, like, expensive jewellery, uh … "

He smiled. "Well, that's just abandonment in disguise."

✕

In post-op, Justin and I count the positives:

I can freak out small children.

Get to catch up on my daytime television.

Less chance that people notice when "the room is too cold" (AKA nipple alert).

Don't have to cook.

An excuse for not exercising.

And, "You weigh less now," he says. "It's like liposuction, without even trying."

"A unilateral breast reduction."

"Just think," he teases, "You'll have an accurate driver's license." He puts socked feet up on the edge of the bed. "When people are bald, do their licenses say, *Hair: bald*?"

Cancer free?

✕

My dad told me once I was named after a friend he met in college, one who had introduced him to my mother's sister, later my aunt, a sort of roundabout introduction to my mother herself.

His name was Leon, he told me.

"Do you still keep in touch?" I'd asked.

"No. No, after college, Leon, uh, he was arrested for drug possession."

"Dad! Really? You hung out with junkies?"

"He wasn't a … Leah, when I knew him … anyway, he was in jail for awhile, and the last I heard, he died of a heart attack."

"In prison?"

"No. Maybe. From my understanding, it was shortly after he got out. Or … shortly before he was supposed to get out? I don't remember."

"And I'm named after this felon?"

He smiled. "Don't tell your mother."

Dear Leelee

I am sincerely sincerely sorry for
(check one)
being a jerk / not listening / being stubborn /
not letting you make enough decisions /
making you make all the decisions / wearing
ugly pants / other _____.

I promise to make it up to you by
(check one)
buying you flowers / bringing you slurpees every
day / spending more time with you / giving
you your space / learning the fine art of
tightrope walking to make you laugh /
other _____.

Tonight for dinner I promise to ~~make~~ order
for you (check one)
pizza / chinese / sushi / a surprise / other _____.

The best football team in the cfl is
(check one)

The Lions / the Argos / the Stamps / the Renegades /
all the others arent even worth mentioning

love love love love love love love love love love love love
your useless boyfriend

Is there an evolutionary basis to cancer? A reason why cells choose to divorce faster than the average North American population? We are being weeded out, the unsuspecting weak.

In younger women, breast cancer is harder to detect. The breasts are still too dense for lumps to be noticed. I picture my dense boobs as stupidly gullible college students, blondly going about their business, napping, cramming for finals, flashing their intoxicated smiles at parties. When it was easy.

><

I throw up into the bowl we used to make popcorn in.

Twice.

><

There was a before that.

At neighbourhood barbecues, I used to eat hot dog buns minus the dog. White bread and mustard, vegetarianism at its most raw, our basset at my feet. My sister, Sabine, liked them with dog, minus mustard, and liked sitting cross-legged, watching our mother rape the neighbour ladies at Nine-Card Brag. My sister was allowed to sit cross-legged because she wasn't playing. If she had been, sitting cross-legged would have been unlucky (according to our mother).

"Bean, get the dog of here," our mother would say, and Chief would smack his lips, beat his tail. "Honeylove," my dad would ask, "want more chips?" and she would shake her head, frown at her cards, shift her chair three times.

><

What I did on my Christmas vacation:

There's me, after a few too many adriamycin cocktails, coiled, cocooned in blue and white bed sheets.

And here's me, eyes practically swollen shut, the week it hurt just to put contacts in, sores on the corners of my mouth as though I'd binged through a bag of salty chips, having just kicked my grandparents out of the room. Is there a commandment: thou shalt not yell at anyone over the age of seventy?

And this one — me, on my left side, the only position where comfort was even remotely possible. You can't see it, but I'm beseeching sleep on the sly, a temporary intoxicating fever, able to block some of it out.

If this is a test, am I allowed to surrender? You win by default.

⋊⋉

The anklet I always wear was an Easter gift I didn't see at first, jokingly attached to a mottled yellow and white bean-bag chick, pinned together at the back of its neck, cutting off the circulation.

Justin was showering with the bathroom door open, humming off-key.

"What should we name it?" I yelled over the spray.

"Omelet."

"Ah. You've given this some thought, have you?"

"No. I'm just clever." He came out of the bathroom, towel-drying his hair. "You know what the word *dry* is in French?"

"What?"

"Sex." He pauses a moment to let this sink in. "You know, it's on your shampoo bottle. For dry hair. *Sex* hair."

"I bet it's not spelled like that. I bet it's not even pronounced like that."

"I bet it is."

He let me not notice the anklet until we were home again, moving Omelet to a perch on the dresser. I undid it slowly, held the thin gold braid up to the light.

"Why didn't you tell me then?" I asked.

"Ruins the fun." He smiled. "I was going to let you go for days."

⋊⋉

Most times, they do both surgeries at once, a two-breasts-with-one-stone sort of deal, cutting out a tumerous mass, adding a clean one. There will never be any absence this way. You supposedly wake up from anesthesia with all the same lines and curves, if perhaps a few more that you can hide beneath bandages, beneath high-necked shirts, marks that will fade with time.

This is what they wanted to do with me, because they didn't understand. There was no point in putting it back just to take it away again.

✂

His is the voice that asks, "You want some water?" Justin waggles a plastic cup. The ice here comes in pellet form, soft. A baby could crush it between its gums. Even the water is designed for the incapacitated. We are the weak, but a cradled, coddled weak, propped with crutches and padded with lambskin, held above toilets and inclined into seating positions. We are never allowed to drop below threshold, pushed passionately from both sides sickwelldeadalive sickwelldeadalive, always in purgatory.

"No."

"Are you sure? You have to stay hydrated, Lee, otherwise —"

"No."

"Fine. You know, sometimes I think you were misdiagnosed. I think you have Crabby Disease." He says this with the gentle cadence of affection, a criticism in a compliment's clothing. "If there is such a thing."

"There *is* such a thing, you idiot; it's called *Krabbe* Disease. It degenerates your nervous system, and then it kills you. The guy down the hall is on chemo for it; you wanna go tell him he has Crabby Disease?"

He stares at me for a moment. "Is nobody allowed to *joke* anymore? Drink the goddamned water!"

ADVANCE DIRECTIVE AND LIVING WILL

I, Leah Isabelle Jordan, being of sound mind, make this statement as a directive to be followed should I become permanently unable to participate in decisions regarding my medical care. These instructions reflect my firm and settled commitment to **refrain** from all medical treatment under the circumstances indicated below. The following instructions apply if I am: a) considered terminal; b) rendered permanently unconscious; or c) have irreversible and/or vegetative brain damage.

I do not want cardiac resuscitation.

I do not want mechanical respiration.

I do not want tube feeding.

I do not want antibiotics.

I do want maximum pain relief.

I do want to

My mother's parents were Christian, and if they visited over a weekend, we all went to church as though we did it every Sunday. Those rare mornings, Bean and I would behave like good little girls who sat still and paid attention, despite not really knowing what was going on.

I liked the way the children's choir sang off-key, and the part where we all pretended we loved each other. The pews smelled deliciously like the pages of my parents' wedding album: stale.

I'm not sure why we stopped going — whether my grandparents were too sick to venture the drive from Lethbridge, or whether everybody just got tired of the charade. Except maybe Sabine, who loved charades. Two words. Second word. Sounds like.

✄

On our way *to* Penticton, Justin and I became trapped in a long line of sterile traffic, 4:30-city-Friday consistency. We clamoured out and paced, kissed on a big rock, and he threatened to pee our initials on it unless we went and found a tree, like, ASAP. Now, on our way home, there are no other cars. I am overheated and irritable, having been curled question mark in the passenger seat for so long. Parallel road runs in either direction.

We get out, I stretch, he does push-ups against the bumper.

"My arms are sore," he notes.

His voice intrudes on the momentary freedom of being more than a foot away from him, away from his nasal hum along with the CBC radio, his twitchy gear-shifting hand, useless to the point of agitation on the incessant highway. "From holding the steering wheel for so long?" I quip.

He flexes. "Only four more hours."

✄

Justin and my dad often visit together, thwarting the time I have to spend alone with the dad who slept away my childhood days and worked away my childhood nights, chasing drunks out of the university and holding back obnoxious concertgoers instead of chasing robbers out of my nightmares and holding my hand. On the days Dad comes by himself, he and

I play hangman. A small victory while tethered to an IV has been my mastery of this game. Wheel of Fortune, here I come.

Today's category is food, which is okay, because my next dose doesn't come until tomorrow, which means today is input and tomorrow is output.

I get _ EM _ N ME _ AN _ _ E _ IE even though Dad spells it wrong (Lemon Meringue Pie), sketch in curls and a bowtie when he gets stumped on _ NC _ I _ A _ A (Enchilada).

"Always guess the E first," I remind him. "It's the most common letter in the English language. RSTLNE."

"Yeah, but you know that. Then you do words like CRAB."

"It has an R in it. And a vowel. Always do the vowels first."

"You said always do E first."

"Well, you know what I mean. It depends on the word. But you have to have some sort of strategy. Guessing Qs and Zs and Js and Ps won't help you."

"It might. Think Pepperoni Pizza. But you would never put that. You're a vegetarian."

"Maybe I want to throw you off," I retort.

Sometimes when they come together, I pretend to be sleeping.

✂

Nausea hides in my shower, waits until I'm not paying attention, grabs me by the shoulders and shakes, sucks the colour from my face, forces me to my knees. Shampoo clings to my hair, clots in clumps.

✂

Justin and I have all the important things in common.

We are both pro-medicine when you're sick, pro-diet soda, pro-spanking, anti-pro wrestling, anti-decaf coffee, and anti-flossing.

We both say see-saw instead of teeter-totter, chicken fingers instead of strips or nuggets, and sked-ule instead of shed-ule.

We are both obsessed with court TV shows and both tend to favour the defendant, will both yell "Mute! Mute!" at the prosecution, even when only minimally provoked. We both, as children, loved dodgeball, and were equally grossed out by the way our peers would wrap Fruit Roll-Ups around their

fingers and suck them until the candy was gone and the dye
had turned their fingers rainbow red blue yellow green.

We both read the Sun, not the Herald, because we like our
news to the point. Which is good, because I could never marry
someone who liked his news drawn out.

✂

My body feels as though it is shutting down, as though
unplugged. My body hums, and stops. My stomach sours.
Kidneys slowly defrost, leaking fluid. My brain warms,
begins to dissolve. Sulci soften. I am perishable. Even if
they manage to save me, I won't be the same.

✂

My dad sleeps curled on the plastic bedside chair, his spine
uncomfortably bent, but all men look at ease when they sleep.
Justin is stretched lengthwise on his stomach on the foot of
my bed, his bare feet brushing the hospital floor, reading his
paycheck.

"They always forget to put my commission on here," he
says. "I sold an LD plasma TV yesterday. A forty-two inch.
Do you know how much those things cost? Like, three grand.
Three and a half grand. They ripped me off, like ..." he men-
tally calculates, "almost two hundred bucks."

"Just call the assistant manager."

"Call the ass man? He's an idiot. He's the one who probably
made this error in the first place. I should have stayed at the
last store; I can't believe all the shit this guy does. I would
have never gotten away with that when I was in his job." When
we started dating, Justin was a so-called "ass man" himself,
at a different Future Shop than the one he's at now, but took
a demotion (and pay cut) in order to transfer closer to our
condo. He figured he'd move back up soon enough.

"Justin," I say, "lower your voice. My dad's asleep."

He grins, sheepishly. "Oops! Hey, wanna dangle his fingers
in a bowl of warm water? Or ..." he grins and holds up my
empty bedpan.

I ignore him, "Speaking of money."

"Yeah?"

"If I die, will you keep or sell the condo?"

"What?" Still holding the bedpan, he looks comical.

"I'm just curious. You probably wouldn't be able to make the payments without my ... meager income. But I was thinking I would want you to sell it anyway, and give my share to charity. You know, whatever was left over after the funeral."

"Okay," he says, "okay, crazy girl, enough." He rolls over onto his back, "Did they switch your meds?"

"We've never talked about it, Justin, I'm serious. I don't really have that much money anyway, just what's in the condo and the car, and a couple grand in savings, you know that. I just thought it would be easier to tell you as opposed to writing the whole thing out, like —"

"No." He pushes himself up onto his feet, paces backwards a few steps.

"Come on, Babe, be realistic."

"No. Leah, it's not —"

My dad arches out of sleep and looks groggily between us. "What's going on?"

"I'm going to get a coffee," Justin says. "Want anything?"

"Yeah," my dad says. "Sure. Just a small, though, black."

When Justin pushes the door shut behind him, my dad shoots me his forged smile. The one that reminds me of the smile he flashed at Bean and me after the divorce, the first time we saw his one-bedroom apartment, the pull-out couch we were to share.

"You're lucky to have him," Dad says.

><

I wonder, what picture will they use? What will they say? Cherished (beloved, treasured?) daughter, sister, girlfriend of ...

Anything else? Was there time for anything else?

Will they lie and say I was courageous?

><

I can't kiss him after eating peanut butter or he'll break out in hives.

The first time Justin told me he was allergic, I thought of those signs at the Y: "There is at least one child on the premises with severe nut allergies. Please refrain from packing or eating products that may contain traces of nuts."

"You're the reason I wasn't allowed to bring M&Ms to swim class."

"Why would you bring M&Ms to swim class?"

For the first time in two years, I crave the gritty thickness. I want it straight, right out of the jar.

My nurse says weird cravings happen when you're on chemo, slips me a vending machine Reese. Later, she remarks, "That's the first thing you've kept down in hours. I think we've found a winner."

✕

Justin still takes pride in his youthful misadventures. How, in third grade, he cut his leg on the chain link fence surrounding his elementary school, making a break for it during recess, intent on seeing whether he could make it to the corner store and back before missing gym. He used masking tape to seal the gash. How he wandered off during a school field trip to the Glenbow Museum, found a direct cab pay phone hanging on a wall, and asked to be taken to the swimming pool, where "his parents would be waiting." How he "borrowed" the money his sister had raised for charity, having spent all weekend starving herself for a World Vision Thirty-Hour Famine. With the money, he informed me, he and a friend of his went for all-you-can-eat wings. How he was misdiagnosed as having ADHD —"and my mom went through a phase where she wouldn't let me have any sugar, except I found a twenty in her wallet and bought 373 sour soothers. Cuz there was GST."

"Sugar doesn't cause ADHD," I told him. This was shortly after we'd moved in together. "It's a myth. It doesn't even make you hyper."

"Where were you in 1992?" he joked.

"I'm tired," I said. "I'm going to take a nap."

He pinched the flesh just over my left hip and smiled affectionately. "Sure, Leelee. Take a nap. How about I fix you a *fiine* meal?"

The condo was quiet, aside from the pulse of my migraine, as he went to get groceries. When I woke up, two hours later, he'd set the table and lit candles, served up a fresh batch of gummy worms, served like a pasta. Their translucent rainbow bodies tangled and scrambled together made me gag.

"And look!" he announced, oblivious, sweeping his arm to gesture towards a massive bowl on the kitchen table, "A marshmallow frog salad." He took my chin between his thumb and forefinger and tweaked it, grinning. "I got inspired."

I don't remember what I felt or if I felt anything at all aside from headache. I remember that he replied, "It was a *joke*," he says, and laughed, perhaps at himself. "I picked up a frozen pizza while you were sleeping. It's in the oven."

"Thank you," I said. "I think I'm going to back to sleep. I still don't feel very —"

"Okay." He cut me off. "Sure. I'll bring you some later."

When he did, I was still awake. He picked a black olive off the top of my slice, popped it in his mouth. He had a pile of folded laundry as well, and put it down on the bed, beside me.

"Feeling better?"

"Sure." I felt grubby, like I had been sleeping in my own skin too long. He left me alone with the pizza and clothing. I shed my work clothes, wriggling out of my cords and unbuttoning my wrinkled blouse. One of his large T-shirts was on top of the pile. He had folded it inside out. I slid it over my naked self, but the iron-on synthetic lettering was cold against my breasts.

⋈

I make the transition from inpatient to outpatient in a wheelchair pushed across the hospital parking lot by Amanda, my sidekick throughout teenagehood, one whose flickering presence lit up when I was diagnosed. I missed her winter wedding, though Justin offered to don a burgundy velvet bridesmaid's dress in my stead. Earlier, he'd threatened to quit his job when they'd insisted he was the only one who could cover the shift of an ill employee.

"And I told them, you want to know about *sick*? My girlfriend will tell you all about being *sick*," he'd ranted this morning, a hurried breakfast run before his shift. He'd tossed me a greasy paper bag of donuts. "You're sure Amanda can do it?"

Amanda has just recently quit smoking. "It was because of you," she tells me, and the wheels of my chair crush parallel lines into the snow. "No more carcinogens in this body."
But earlier she'd waved a grainy black and white ultrasound image at me, so excited I couldn't make out what was and was not embryo.

She is jittery as she guides me into the passenger seat of her car.

"I'm sorry," she says, as her fingers fumble to put the keys into the ignition. "I'm still not sleeping well, because of, you know, um ... cravings. I'm sorry, I can't ... I can't concentrate. I'm just *dying* for a cigarette."

><

A new study or a new joke?

Is there anything that doesn't cause cancer?

Barbecues (carcinogens) cell phones (radio waves) Teflon (chemical compounds) farmed salmon (PCB) soya sauce high-voltage power lines birth control asbestos antiperspirant dandruff shampoo prescription skin cream tanning beds mouthwash too much sun too little sun pesticides x-rays stress hair dye red dye cholesterol pills TV tap water animal fat bras?

And, apparently, the alloy in certain bullets, if imbedded in the skin. Because, please, don't shoot me, I might get cancer!

><

They give me tamoxifen to prevent recurrence, a pamphlet on side effects to prevent me from asking questions. Weight gain, lack of energy, mood swings, and painful intercourse. But, should you manage to get in the mood despite being fat, lazy, temperamental, and in pain, our good friend Tammy will likely lower your chances of getting pregnant.

"But you should still be using protection, if you don't want to get pregnant. And, like it says, the birth control pill or any other hormonal method involving estrogen should not be used for women who've had breast cancer."

Actually, it says, *the birth control pill or any other hormonal method involving estrogen should not be used for women who've had* **beast** *cancer.* An apt typo, if I do say so myself.

(29

⋊

There was one day during the first year of our relationship — I don't know when, except that it was snowing, which, in Calgary, doesn't really rule out any date in particular — that we decided we wanted a baby. We were both so enraptured with this idea, however last minute it was (aroused by a pair of tiny Nikes on display outside a Toys "R" Us), that even afterwards we could not both stop sprouting reasons why our plan was so inspired.

"And even if we break up," I said, "it won't be like my parents. Because we're always going to be friends, you know, either way."

Justin rolled over. "What?"

"Well, you know. Because we're —"

"Jesus, Leah!" He got up then, naked, and walked out of the room, passing right in front of the window.

"Hey, oh, come on, don't —"

⋊

After coming home from the hospital, I don't want him to touch me. His hands, like everybody's hands, feel like rubber, poking, prodding, cupping, massaging. The first few times I unzip my skin and wait in the corner, watching a body that isn't mine. A human buffet. Take what you want and ignore the rest.

⋊

I take Justin's little niece and her friend to the park, and we all pile onto one tire swing until my nausea insists on getting up there with us, all elbows and knees, jabbing me in the gut. As a child, I perversely cherished stomach aches, the permission to confine oneself to bed surrounded by towels. Stomach aches were even more exotic in their rarity. While I could, and frequently did, experience motion sickness nausea for something as little as watching TV upside down, verified flus that actually threatened vomiting were few and far between. Rarer still was a vomit story from my mother's own childhood, an anomalous excerpt, in which she threw up off the top bunk, missing her siblings, but forever tainting a stuffed koala. I loved this story, loved the opportunity to hear it, clutching my own parachuted towel to my face.

If you wish too hard for something, does it come true?

✂

dis·eased dizēzd *adj.* **1** affected with disease. **2** unsound or disordered.

de·ceased di'sēst *adj.* **1** dead.

✂

Apparently, only people missing large chunks of cerebral matter would *ever* blow-dry jeans.

"You're using the blow-dryer? What's wrong with the regular dryer?"

"Nothing, this way is just quicker. Plus, the dryer's coin-op."

"There's no way it's faster." Justin leans over, feels for dampness on the jeans I have stretched in the shape of an inverted v on the carpet.

"Don't touch my clothes!"

"Ooh, *don't touch my clothes!*"

"Are you done yet?"

"Are you done yet?"

"You're five, you know that?"

"You're five, you know that?"

"Are the washers at our new place coin-op?"

"Do you want fifty cents?"

"Hey, big spender."

"We're going to be late."

"Just as soon as my pants dry."

✂

When I was eight, Adelaide Kaltenbach, who was number five out of ten kids, and whose grandparents were visiting from Germany at the time, drowned in the community pool.

My mother knew certain things about Adelaide's mother and consequently so did I. For example, that she didn't work, and that she baked ("You know, you don't have to be a stay-at-home mom to bake for your bloody kids!"), and that she loved being pregnant ("You'd *have* to love being pregnant to do it for fifteen years straight!"). The oldest, number one, was fourteen, and they were all home schooled, which I found baffling. How did Adelaide's mother, perpetually pregnant and baking, raise and teach ten children?

My big sister, Bean, was at the pool that day, and then came home, her hair stringy, tiny wet circles marking preteen breasts on the front of her T-shirt. She said, "One of those Christian kids *died* today, she drowned, the middle girl!"

Later, I heard my mother tell my dad that Adelaide's mom probably cut her hair while she was pregnant, which was bad luck. I wondered about my own mother, whose hair was page-boy short as far back as high school.

And then, what could have been no less than a week later, they told us about the divorce, which they said, without looking at each other, was not our fault. Maybe they thought after Adelaide Kaltenbach drowning, we wouldn't think it was that bad.

Bad news congregates, spawns, spreads, prompts clichés about Murphy's Law and raining/pouring. Bad news means more bad news.

><

When he sleeps, he's a pillow thief, a blanket kicker, an arm flailer. I wake up with his hand splayed across my rib cage, his thumb touching the edge of my scar.

><

The morning my cat dies, Justin is busy, I am busy, we are both late because the cat didn't lick our eyes open, do his superstitious sprint down the stairs ahead of me, loop twice around his food dish, and put his paws up on my leg in orgasmic breakfast bliss as I run the can opener. Eightball has been waking me up since I moved in with my dad shortly after starting high school, then palm-of-my-hand small, pocket-of-my-housecoat small. During the weeks I spent hospitalized, Eightball shunned his litter box and left Justin presents in the bathtub.

A cardboard shoebox that once held what Justin referred to as my "hooker boots" seems too tacky to be an eternal sun-spot. I can't put the lid on. Eightball stares at me, his unleavened body petrified. I pull at my nubby hair, twist it around my fingers, tug, fray.

"Did you bury the cat yet?" Justin wants to know.

"Eightball," I say. "Not *the cat*."

✂

Some time after Adelaide died, I saw her mother sitting crookedly on a bench at the back of Safeway, nursing number eleven. She still had long hair, which I always thought was unusual for a mother, but liked. Number eleven was draped sluggishly across its mother's lap, barely sucking on her large, exposed breast, pulpy and tracked with thick, purple veins.

I had been shooed from my own mother, having been told to locate an onion.

I wonder if somebody asked how many kids they had, if they would say eleven, or if they would just say ten. Maybe this baby was a new number ten, and all the kids after Adelaide just moved up in the ranks. Maybe there was a new number five.

✂

But ... there is ... I mean, one day I am ... I mean, I feel ... feel like going out and buying sheets as far away from the crisp barely blue of hospital. And I do, giant retro lime green and pink checkers, swooping white half circles, fuzzy Muppet-skin marshmallow teenage pillows. I spend $248.49 that I don't have.

✂

breast·ed brest'ed *v.* **tr. 1** to rise over; climb.

breast·ing brest'ing *v.* **tr. 1** to encounter

or advance against resolutely.

)(two

When I was eleven, cancer and I ran into each other in a veterinary office, although I wasn't really sure if it was her or not. Our vet said that the mammary sized mass under our dog's jaw was quite possibly an abscess. While we were in the process of deciding whether or not to have it removed, biopsied, or lanced, Chief decided for us by having a grand finale seizure under the kitchen table.

There was this boy I dated in high school, one who I then referred to as my "first love." One day he took me back to his house and taught me how to play beach volleyball in the backyard. I only mention this because, oddly enough, his house, where he'd lived since he was a fetus, was next door to that of a childhood friend. For years, I ran around in her backyard in dress-up clothes ten times too big, ignoring any kids next door. I'm sure there must have been some form of contact between me and my future love interest, though neither of us remembered any. Obviously not love at first sight.

It seems it was not that way with cancer and me either.

✂

After a week of boredom, I feel healthy enough to venture out on my own. The Kensington Starbucks enthralls me the way I, as a child, was thrilled by art galleries. A chai frappuccino seeps flavour into the beads on my tongue, an extraordinary ordinary. I choose a lounge chair and stare out the window behind a chalky proclamation drawn onto the glass, as a downpour begins almost instantly, causing passersby to flood into the tiny shop, placing hurried orders for hot drinks.

✂

A psychic named Claudia tells me over avocado and cream cheese sandwiches that this isn't how I will die. She also tells me I will marry an Italian hunchback and asserts that I am good with my hands. Good at detecting lumps. At the end of this eighty-five dollars, she hands me a business card and says, "Call me later, Laura." I think, *I remembered your name, and I don't have supernatural powers.*

><

Once, during a particularly angsty bout of teenagehood, Sabine stole all the tampons from my purse. This was three and a half days after the boy I liked performed a song during a school pep rally, a sort of wah-wah rock 'n' roll song with another girl's name in it. I went down into the ravine behind our house and sat with my feet in the stream for a long time, twiddling the sludgy leaves with my toes.

I remember being totally eight-tenths of the way to killing myself.

><

Six days after my twenty-fifth birthday, my GP kicks off our follow-up with a belated, slightly deflated, foil balloon. But she is the one with the results. I have forgiven her long ago for her Stage III tardiness, her ability to wait. I, on the other hand, book the first appointment of the day, up so early I don't even bother with the fake boob Justin nicknamed Christina, do not care that I'm up at seven o'clock on my day off. I wait for no one anymore.

><

Theirs were the voices that said I was spending too much time with him, that suggested (rhetorically) that being with only one person all the time was unhealthy, wasn't it? That said I wasn't like this with my other boyfriends.

I want to know, "What other boyfriends?" Are they refer-ring to my sporadic crushes, my one-sided infatuations?

They say I'm going to want them to be there when we break up.

"*When* we break up?"

><

Sometimes I wake up to doorbells. Sometimes at four-thirty in the morning, in the middle of dreams in which I live underwater, in which my surgical team is joined by my child-hood pediatrician, his sour parmesan cheese smell I'd grown to associate with all doctors. No matter where or when, there are people ringing my bell. Sometimes I still go look through my peephole. In the hospital, I peered out the window down onto the parking lot below.

✕

Justin buries me in the sand of Okanagan Beach. He sculpts a fake body, adds a set of mammoth breasts. Cold and damp beneath my new cleavage, I feel strangely proportional. This is the first vacation we have been able to afford.

I nuzzle my head in against one of his sandalled feet, "We should move here."

"We should move here?"

I crane my neck. The sun has slipped behind a craggy cloud. "Why not? You don't think we could use a change of pace? Here I have two breasts."

"Are you kidding?" he demands.

"Twenty-three percent," I say. "I'm getting more and more attached to this idea."

"What about your … your treatments? Your doctors? You can't just up and … Jesus, Leah."

I lick my lips, dry with heat. "Aww, you're no fun. Why can't I be spontaneous? Why can't I be *happy*?"

His is the voice that says, "I don't want you happy! I want you *alive*!"

I scramble out of the grit, suddenly claustrophobic. The sand cleaves around me, empty, a fault line.

✕

There was no history of cancer in our family. None. Even our smoking relatives, those who smoked while eating, while holding grandbabies on their laps, while on the toilet — even they succumbed to emphysema first.

✕

I drive home from Starbucks later than I intended, fumbling with my keys as the rain spills off the crest above the condo door and into my patchy hair.

Justin, inside, with a towel draped around his neck but otherwise clad only in a pair of boxers, stands up but doesn't approach me. His gaze, however, stalks over and gets up in my face, daring to slap me. I don't think I've ever seen him this angry. But it is tough to take him seriously, the waistband of his shorts rolled over a few times at his hips, his wet hair and eyelashes spiked like the points of stars. Justin, I've come to realize, buys L underwear for reasons similar to why females squeeze into XS shirts and size 0 jeans.

"I. Walked. Home," he informs me, each word its own biting sentence. "All the way from the *freakin'* bus stop. In this goddamned downpour. Where were you?"

"I ... didn't do it on purpose. I forgot. Honestly." This is the truth. "Why didn't you call a cab?"

He slams his whole body down onto the couch, and a dinner plate he's left on the opposite end vibrates with the motion of the cushions. A pile of what he calls "scalp" potatoes, spread thick with dark yellow mustard, slips off and falls to the carpet. We look at this mess, simultaneously, but neither of us moves.

"I called *you*," he says, "about a hundred times. I was worried. Now I'm just pissed. And don't you *dare* play the cancer card."

I feel my cheeks deepen with an undifferentiated flush. Emotions all stem from the same hot yolk within, a spike in adrenaline, primal, no matter what the end result. Anger. Embarrassment. Excitement.

✂

Hers is the same voice that asks me to make an appearance at a breast cancer support group.

"I don't need support."

"Everybody needs support, Leah. But actually, I meant it more for them than for you. The group members, I mean. I recommended you to the facilitator. She'd like you to give a talk to some of the newly diagnosed patients, tell them what to expect. It's totally up to you, though."

Sure, I want to say, *when you want something from me...*

And even then, what would I say? Tell them what to expect?

Expect to get absorbed in daytime television shows in which preteen couples compete to see who can outperform the others by dancing the cha cha. Expect to start eating with plastic cutlery, because even the taste of metal will linger in your mouth for hours. Expect to develop puffy chipmunk cheeks, swollen childlike fingers, pregnant lady ankles. Expect to feel as though you have become a thermostat — checked, adjusted, and then abandoned. Expect to … expect to hate.

✕

"Do you want me to drive for awhile?"

Justin looks at me incredulously, *"No."*

I fold and refold the Okanagan map in my hands, blue river veins. As a child, I would repeat my own name over and over until it sounded foreign on my tongue. Maybe it can work backwards too — if I say ex-boyfriend enough, it will start to sound familiar.

After a moment, he turns the volume on the radio down. "Are we … I mean … the condo only has one bedroom. If we're *broken up*," he lets go of the wheel and hooks his fingers into air quotes around these last two words. This is a foreign tongue for him too, and he stumbles over what he wants to say next. "I mean, well, we can't really … am I going to look for a place, or are you?"

I turn the volume on the radio up.

"Leah …"

I will be the one looking. One should always be on the lookout.

✕

How to argue correctly:

Don't bring up past history.

Don't bring third parties into your arguments.

Don't name call.

Don't interrupt your partner.

Don't blame or accuse your partner.

Don't use statements starting with "you;" rather, use statements starting with "I."

And this, the coup de grâce, the one that cracks us both up:

Try to hold hands with your partner while arguing to make you feel closer.

Leah Jordan, BA
lijord@ucalgary.ca

Objective

To achieve financial independence from my father
and (ex?) boyfriend; to be a normal, functioning
member of society.

Experience

2004 – 200? [NW Calgary]

- Breast Cancer Patient
- Stage IIB, unilateral mastectomy
- Proficient at a wide variety of chemotherapies
- Currently expert in tamoxifen, short hairdos,
  and missed work days

2001 – 200? [NW Calgary]

- Testing Administrator / Supervisor
- Responsible for administration and supervision
  of individuals writing standardized exams
  (GRE, MCAT, LSAT, etc.) that I would personally fail
- Currently declared "disabled" (AKA unable to hand
  people paper and watch them write)

Education

1998 – 2002 [NW Calgary]

- University of Calgary
- BA Communications and Culture
- AKA certified to do absolutely nothing

How many times have I heard, *you're lucky*?

"You're lucky you get disability from your job."

"You're lucky your mortgage is low."

"You're lucky this didn't happen when you were still in school!"

"You're lucky you caught this as early as you did."

"You're lucky you don't live in the States."

And some, the few who know, will remind me how lucky I am that my dad had savings accounts for both me and Bean, in case of trauma. I think he was thinking robbery, or fire, or losing our jobs. They don't understand. Having backups was supposed to make it never happen. That account was not *in case* something ever happened to me, it was to *prevent* anything from happening to me. With it I was supposed to be safe.

⤬

We pull up in front of the house, and the claustrophobic Okanagan haze is gone, the air still with an Albertan autumn. My suitcase falls from the backseat onto the floor of the car with the sudden stop in momentum. We are broken up. We look out opposite windows. Along the driveways across the street, distended plastic trash bags wait to be collected come morning. I will call my dad tomorrow, ask if he wants to have haggis after my checkup.

⤬

It snowed on the night of my high school graduation dinner-dance, causing us girls — applying body glitter, shaving our armpits, adjusting corsages — to freak out. In retrospect, though, the picture of us all in rubber boots with our satin domed dresses hiked up around our knees, tromping across the field with our backs to the camera, is the best picture I have of the night. Not the one with my parents posed awkwardly on either side of me, a gaping space of background drapery over my head and between the two that would cause any professional photographer to cringe. Nor still the one of my date eating chicken, with an unfortunate orange fleck (carrot?) in his teeth. I like how we all look, going off into a world where being fully dignified is impossible.

✂

Justin's sister prefers snail mail to e-mail. Her most recent letter arrives just over a week after our return.

Hey you two!

If you've got this, you're probably back from your trip. I hope the rest and relaxation treated you well. You both deserve it. We are well and good here, as is your crazy little niece. You'll be happy to know that all the children at her school did the Terry Fox run on Thursday. It just brightens my heart to see everybody helping out. Anyway, afterwards she came home and told me, "Guess what, Mom? I did the Tony Fox run for cancelled people today. I'm so glad I could help so those poor people don't have to get cancelled anymore!"

P.S. Leah, thanks to you, I never forget my monthly BSE.

I wonder if he's told her now, told anyone, actually, that we're not together anymore. Do I know him well enough to assume he has not?

✂

Justin insists on accompanying me to work the day the car doors refuse to open, frozen shut overnight. Companionship, he claims, will dull the agony of the eleven-minute walk from our condo to the train station, and then the thirteen-minute walk from the train stop to my office. We take turns helping

(41

each other on with our winter paraphernalia. He draws a scarf around my face, pulling it tight around my mouth, pulling my zipper up to the collar to constrict it into place.

We tromp through snow, knee-deep; our parkas crinkle and snap with cold as we move, too indifferent to speak. We huddle under the pitiful heat offered by the station's shelter.

"One time," Justin says, his voice stifled behind his scarf, "when I was, like, maybe six or seven, there was a snowstorm like this, but school wasn't closed. My mom kept us home anyway and jacked the heat up in the house, put my sister and me in bathing suits, and made lemonade."

"Let's do that now," I say, but a train rushes down the tracks, sucking the wind and my words along with it.

✕

As a child, I never did anything dangerous, unless talking on the phone or organizing events for student council are considered precarious hobbies. Even younger, I always wore my helmet while biking, shied ungracefully away from sports teams and horseback riding, instead making giant abstract finger paintings in the basement. All I did was catch a white moth and bring it into the house, spend my babysitting money on a bouquet of red and white roses for one of my mother's birthdays, stitch appliqués onto the pocket of my jeans without taking them off. Things that disobeyed my mother's strange set of rules, ominous messages written into perky rhymes that my brain recited like the stubborn lyrics to a song that you can't get out of your head. But maybe I did all those things on purpose.

✕

Justin helps me move, rents a truck, insists on paying, brings a root beer Slurpee, asks "And you met this guy where?" in reference to my new landlord.

"I haven't *met* him; he's the cousin of a guy my dad knows." I don't tell him that once I mentioned having (had?) cancer over the phone, the guy offered to include utilities. Under the guise of needing to rent the place quickly, of course.

He frowns, "Funny, your dad never mentioned him."

"You still talk to my ..." I say, but catch myself. "Never mind."

"Well … Jesus! What's wrong with —"

"I said *never mind*." The Slurpee ice turns white around my straw, sucked clean of syrup.

We make nice with my new landlord while Justin heaves boxes and I unpack my things in the basement.

"I'm Andrew," this man, who I will be living under, introduces himself.

"Leah. You're a teacher, my dad said?" A teacher, and he's my age.

"Yeah. Sixth grade. Right now we're doing, you know, synonyms, antonyms, homonyms …"

"Homonyms?"

"Words that have the same sound and sometimes the same spelling but different meanings. Like, uh … period. Punctuation at the end of a sentence. Menstrual cycle. A certain length of time. Sequence of atomic elements."

"Impressive."

I follow Justin to the truck when he goes back for more boxes. I am thinking about how behind I am, in the grand scheme of growing up. Andrew is my age and is doing something with his life, something he actually *wants* to do. Cancer really takes you out of the running.

"I don't like this guy," Justin says.

"Why? Can you hold onto that lid? You're about to have books all over the sidewalk."

"Oh, come on, what kind of guy says menstrual cycle?"

"Justin!"

"I just got weird vibes from him."

"You got weird vibes from him?"

"Look," he says, "Just be careful, okay? Period."

✕

I dream I'm pushing my sister in a stroller, her long, teenaged legs bent awkwardly, sandaled feet dragging on the sidewalk. Her stomach hurts, she is whining. She's saying *she's* sick.

can·cer kansər *n.* **1** any of various malignant neoplasms characterized by the proliferation of anaplastic cells that tend to invade surrounding tissue and metastasize to new body sites. **2** the fourth sign of the zodiac in astrology, between Leo and Gemini. **3** a pernicious, spreading evil.

✄

My mother aspired to be, but never became, a dentist. Instead, she worked at Canada Olympic Park, giving tours, gesturing vehemently at the luge track and the ski jumps when ESL patrons were visiting. According to her, this was a stepping stone.

She always scheduled my dental checkups on days she could take me, but ignored my slobbery, drooling questions about when the freezing would wear off, asking the hygienists about their schooling. At night, she would wash her red work shirt and lament her inability to speak French and Mandarin.

"I'm going to buy one of those tapes and listen to it when I'm driving."

✄

An itchy nose means you will have a quarrel with someone.

Marry in April when you can, joy for maiden & for man.

A howling dog foretells the death of someone nearby.

She who can walk through a swarm of bees without being stung is a virgin.

The spouse who goes to sleep first on the wedding night will be the first to die.

If you get interrupted while making your bed, you will have a restless sleep.

A child born between the old and new moons is fated to die young.

Thursday's child has far to go.

Steponacrack, breakyourmothersback.

⊰

They are my age, these voices that verify their names and addresses, ask me for extra pencils, let me know when they need to take a break. I watch them on the black and white video monitor, clicking keys and filling in Scantron bubbles, snapping their heads towards the clock every five or so minutes. I say nothing when a girl glances a little too long at the desk beside her. I forget to bring scrap paper by at the thirty-minute mark. I ignore the standardized orange HB pencils, dull and cracked from use, begging to be sharpened.

Another line that divides the before and after, my indifference at work, but not just at work. If she, she who holds up my CT scans, who makes pleasant chatter about her two kids while molding my remaining breast like playdough, if she can afford it, then so can I.

Is Your Relationship In Trouble?

Check the box if you would answer "true" to the statement.

- ☑ My partner and I often go to sleep without having resolved disagreements.
- ☐ I often don't think my partner is trying.
- ☑ My partner is unaware of some of my most important desires, interests, and preferences.
- ☑ I find it difficult to express my deepest feelings to my partner.
- ☑ When it comes to finances, my partner and I usually cannot agree on how to set priorities.
- ☐ My partner is no longer attracted to me physically.
- ☐ I find myself expressing my affections for my partner more than my partner does.
- ☐ My partner is not the same person he/she was when we first began dating.
- ☐ The problems in my relationship are my partner's fault.
- ☑ My sex life with my partner is disappointing.
- ☐ My partner is aware that I am consulting material to help me understand our circumstances.
- ☑ I often feel that my partner doesn't really know who I am.

⊰

Jordan. After you. It doesn't matter what sex it is. That way
we don't have to hyphenate, but it'll be like it still has your
last name."

I didn't tell him I want kids named Genevieve and Sierra.

"What's wrong with hyphenating?"

"My grandma's neighbour had a hyphenated last name.
Her name was like, Evelyn Brown-Claw. I went to her funeral,
and everyone kept saying, 'God bless Mrs. Brown-Claw. Poor,
poor, Mrs. Brown-Claw.'"

"So? What does that have to do with anything? Jordan
sounds fine with your last name."

"Exactly. Which is why we should just leave it like that. Just
Jordan."

⊰

My dad insists on paying my car insurance. "For now, Leah,
just for now."

I say, "No."

"It's just temporary. You do my laundry, and we'll call it a deal."

"No. I'll just take the train to work. I already do that, sometimes, it's not even that far ... and I'm only part time, anyway.
The walk is ..."

We both know, though, that I won't (take the train) and
that I will (let him pay), and that I won't (like it) and that I
will (accept it) and that I do (need it) and that I will (do his
laundry).

⊰

When I am married, we will go to my grandparents' for
Thanksgiving, and my husband will insist on driving. He
will eat too much off the cheese platter, because he will
have to try all the different cheeses, and then try them
again. Then our daughter will eat too much off the cheese
platter, and try to compensate by drinking too much water.
Our daughter will be the kind of kid who, when we tell her
to be careful about lice, will start checking the heads of
all the other kids at school for little white bugs. This will
make us wonder if perhaps we should put off telling her
about sex.

We will come home, and our daughter will throw up near, but not in the toilet. She will tell me how much she hates me, in those exact words, "I hate you," and my husband will close all the cupboards and say, "Why don't you ever close the cupboards? One of these days I'm going to whack my head into one and get brain damage."

✂

boob boōb *n.* 1 informal either of two soft fleshy milk-secreting glandular organs on the chest of a woman.

2 slang one who is ignorant, stupid, or naïve. 3 *v. tr.* to commit a faux pas or a fault or make a serious mistake.

✂

The scraping of chair legs against hardwood floor.

The muffled asynchrony of dissimilar voices.

The simultaneous scuttle of laughter and dice. Or laughter and ice.

Upstairs, it appears, Andrew is having a party, one that creeps like a liquid along the floorboards, through the cracks, and down my apartment walls.

My workout clothes are too loose on my frame, and clump around my hips and at my shoulders. I twist the excess clothing in front of the mirror, securing it off with an elastic. It reminds me of Sabine's sweaters tied off into knots at her hips, at her breastbone, the height of 80s fashion. I am still too nauseous to start running again, but I don't want to be in this house anymore.

At the top of the stairs, I run into Andrew, gripping a solid, bulging bag of trash.

"Leah! Hey!"

"Hi."

"How's it going?"

"Not bad."

He shifts the garbage to his other hand. "I'm sorry, were we being too noisy? I was just having a couple of my co-workers over for a few drinks."

"Oh, no, no, don't worry about it."

He cocks his head to the side, "You know, if you're not doing anything, you should join us. We're just having drinks. Low key."

"Oh …" My skin itches behind the stretched nylon fabric. "Um … well, I'm all sweaty, and stuff. I was just working out."

"Big run?"

"Um, well, medium sized."

"I should start again." Andrew sets the garbage down. The bag sags and changes shape with the pressure of the concrete. "Well, why don't you take a shower and just pop in when you're done? No rush."

Water fills the tub and dampens the clamour of Andrew's upstairs guests. Frivolous and not paying attention, I receive a cold shock when I climb in. I pull the stopper and hold my fingers near the drain, feeling the suction of water escaping.

⋇

They, that is, my parents, used to shuffle us back and forth between them on the c-train, a vortex that whooshed us from sw to nw or nw to sw. I liked to sit in the seats facing the opposite direction from where we were going. It made me feel pulled rather than pushed.

⋇

New homes come with old treasures. My first time living on my own, fresh out of high school, my roommates and I were blessed with an old game of Monopoly, among other things. Bathroom faucets labelled backwards. Light bulbs reminiscent of a dental office. A furnace that hadn't been cleaned in two years, puffing dusty smoker's breath through the vents in winter. My single suite is idiosyncratic, but not in the quirky way my university pad was. My toilet appears to have an eating disorder, sometimes refusing to flush, other times vomiting its contents. The walls refuse to hold my posters and routinely drop them, terrifyingly, on my face at night. The shower pours only cold water for the first two minutes, until I've cranked the hot faucet as far as it will go, and then, accompanied by a ferocious scream, the hot rushes in. Twice,

I've leapt out, clutching a patch of flushed purple skin, so hot I am pulsing.

Home is not where the heart is. At least not this home, angry at me for no reason. Or, at least, a reason I have yet to determine.

✕

I have only ever been to one funeral, an eighty-seven-year-old great-aunt on my mother's side, one I'd met only a few times. I was in my final year of university, just days from final exams. She died of liver failure, but this was not mentioned on her funeral card. Also not mentioned on her funeral card — she was a neat freak (my mother has vivid memories of her plastic couch covers and guest bedroom sheets worn thin from being washed too many times). She was an unlikely gardener, with an indoor row of incessantly thriving gardenia. At age fifteen, she almost died of pneumonia. One room in her house was wallpapered with the recurring blank stare of a Raggedy Ann doll. She left all her belongings to her church, aside from a stamp collection, which she left to a neighbour none of her relatives had heard of.

These things are all important.

✕

The scar where my breast used to be tingles. The phantom boob. In the mirror, I realize I can now pull my lesbian hair back into the stubby beginnings of a ponytail.

Cancer and Spirituality

Finding out one has cancer is both difficult and life-changing. Those diagnosed are often forced to re-evaluate their priorities and reorganize their perceptions of the world in the face of potentially life threatening conditions. Spirituality is often part of this journey.

Many believe that faith and hope can significantly impact the way patients deal with a cancer diagnosis. Some evidence has shown prayer to be linked with better health outcomes and emotional well-being, especially when patients know they are being prayed for. It is thought that knowing others are praying for you for may instill greater hope in those suffering from illness.

Spirituality has also been linked to hope for patients and their families in terms of the afterlife. Psychological benefits of the belief that, after death, individuals are happy, protected, and reunited with their loved ones include decreased stress and fear.

The way one expresses spirituality is intensely personal, and varies from individual to individual. It may include organized religion, participation in church services, books or literature, prayer, meditation, and ritual. Regardless of the way patients choose to direct their spirituality, many say its presence has been invaluable, both in their recovery, and in their lives long-term.

In Justin's absence, I recycle. I take the large slabs of cardboard and bend and distort them, send them down the chute,
where they fall up against each other at awkward angles. Next,
the cans, ribbed metal, rinsed of their insides. In the bag they
are all anonymous, stripped of their labels. These I throw in
all at once, too apathetic to cut off their ends and flatten them
properly. I rip coil bindings from old, half filled notebooks.
The springs go into METAL, the pages into PAPER.

I save the glass for last. On a good day, the bin is already
half full. That way, you can hear the smash.

I take the C-train to Fish Creek and sit at the bus stop,
watching the gawky maneuvering of buses pulling in and
out, the slow hiss of the doors opening and shutting for
passengers. Somehow, the knowledge that I am only one
ride away from my sister and yet don't have to see her is
comforting. I walk along the line of yellow squares, the
do-not-cross line, on the station platform. Their patterned
bumps remind me of Lego. Of building castles, beauty par-
lours. Of building walls.

✕

A counsellor my father took me to shortly after my parents'
divorce made me lie across the floor and taught me progressive muscle relaxation and imagery as a way of calming my
anxiety. At the time I couldn't see how squeezing my fists
until my palms began to tingle, scrunching my eyes shut until
I could see globs like microbes swarming behind my lids, was
going to help me relax.

"Empty your mind, Leah," she told me, and with my eyes
closed, I could not tell where in the room her voice was coming from. "Your whole body is relaxed. Feel every last bit of
tension drain from your body. You are light. You are free from
worry. What do you feel like?"

I felt like I was falling through the open floor.

✕

Andrew invites me upstairs for dinner, and beside my plate
is a real cup. Not plastic, not one he can throw out. Once, at
a dinner party shortly after I was discharged, we raised our
glasses for a toast and it was then that I realized mine was the

only one that wouldn't clink. Ignorance is contagious. But this is real stemware.

"I shouldn't show you this," Andrew says, and my eyes are drawn away from the place settings. "Ethically. Legally. But it's just too funny." The piece of paper he comes back with is lined, smudged with childish pencil print. "I asked them to write about what they did last summer," he says, adding the disclaimer, "God, what a stereotypical teacher thing to do."

Last summer my brother and I got a tramp. My mom said our family could finely afford one. my brother and I would take turns jumping on the tramp because it is dangerous to go on together. Sometimes we would stay up late jumping because we liked the tramp so much.

The laughter that follows feels like sex, squeezing my abdominal muscles.

"I've read it like, six times, and it's still funny," he admits.

"My dad helped us pick the tramp," I mock, *"He said it was the nicest tramp of all."*

"It was a second-hand tramp," Andrew adds. *"It was cheap!"*

✂

After I am divorced, but not too long after, when we are still paying hideous lawyer bills and fighting for custody over twelve-dollar potted plants, our daughter will play a game at school in which she, fully supervised, will compete to see how many marshmallows she can fit in her mouth at once, while still retaining the ability to say "Fuzzy Bunny."

This, however, will result in her requiring CPR, a visit to the emergency room. Pink liquid pumped out of her lungs.

And, furthermore, this will be my fault, or so my ex-husband will say. My brain will play the saxophone solo from "I Will Always Love You" when he says this.

"She doesn't feel *loved*. She doesn't feel like you *want* her. I told you, you should have breastfed."

✂

The first cold since. That first slippery, middle-of-the-night, back-of-the-throat itchiness. The thick inhale, slice of larynx. I marvel at its ability to incapacitate me, leave me begging for the saccharine syrups of childhood. Have I not

heaved and snivelled and writhed my way through worse?
Sacrificed pieces of my flesh, of my soul?

And yet, I am still reduced to melodrama, to rolls of toilet
paper slowly unravelling.

Do I call my doctor, or rather, her assistant, wait for the
call back, listen to calmly recited facts about white blood cell
counts and Vitamin c?

Or, my dad? Or?...

✂

There are only a few things that I have retained — *really*
retained, that is, from my childhood. Or, more precisely,
a few *objects* I have retained from my childhood. In com-
parison to the *things* I have retained, the *objects* are few. A
slab of thickly pencilled sketches, their smudgy shadows
on the backs of the pages before them. A jewellery box of
dehydrated, preserved turkey wishbones. I unpack these
items knowing I will only have to pack them again, push
them to the back of my closet, out of range of possible
embarrassment.

Amongst these, a rare find, a box of sculpted soap figu-
rines, a collection that ended promptly upon my discovery
that some soaps were made of whale blubber. The figures are
gummed together with deflated bath beads, the cardboard
beneath them dark with oil. A triceratops' front horn is
chipped and dented, a fairy's wing torn.

I take Puss 'n Boots, climb into the bathtub, let the water
swirl around me into the grimy basin, rub his smiling face
against my muted thighs, my arms, my breast, until his
grinning face is wiped clean.

)(three

With the nauseating freedom of being single, I go to church. There is no reason behind my picking a church other than its proximity to my home. I don't remember which denomination we'd been to when I was younger, but I surprise myself by remembering lyrics to some of the songs, even those that aren't in English. *Manducat dominum / Pauper, pauper / Servus et humilis.*

There are children with glittery crafts who disappear downstairs for the majority of the service; elderly patrons hugging ventilators down the aisle; floral sweaters shaped like mothers with infants slung over their shoulders; prematurely balding men with faces shockingly young; a hideously obese woman, folds of flesh spilling out from the armholes of her sleeveless blouse, a gaudy engagement ring cutting off the circulation on the fourth finger of her left hand.

A naivety I recognize, the belief that you are invulnerable.

A girl whose brown hair is pulled severely into a ponytail that grazes the hollow of her back and whose face reminds me of Adelaide's. A sister? I wonder. The Kaltenbachs were religious, or must have been. You don't pop out that many babies unless you know God is going to put you in time out if you use condoms. Adelaide would have gotten a free pass to a kick-ass afterlife, having Jesus in her genes and all. If you get to design your own heaven, I bet in hers she would have her own bedroom. And maybe a ball pit. I try not to think about mine. It's better not to get your hopes up.

"Please keep the sick and dying in your prayers," the priest says, and recites their names. "Jenny Stratton. Olga Stamninski. Peter Craig. Samuel Mennit. Josie Feedler-Wayburn."

miss mis *n.* **1** used as a courtesy title before the surname or full name of a single girl or woman. **2** *v.* **tr.** to fail to hit, reach, catch, meet, or otherwise make contact with. **3** *v.* **intr.** to feel the lack or loss of.

✂

Funny how I only see things one way now. The one way, the cancer way, a mild but persuasive force that takes me by the shoulders and points me in the same direction over and over. A what if.

What if blood in my urine isn't a simple UTI, but is a sign of spread to my ovaries? What if forgetting my swipe card for work is a sign of spread to my brain, rather than just ordinary carelessness? What if this unshakable irritability is irreversible chemo side effects masquerading as PMS?

✂

As a child, I sometimes wondered whether, if Adelaide Kaltenbach hadn't died, would we one day have become friends? In my version of our friendship, Adelaide would not have been home-schooled. I pictured her name beside mine on book report title pages and on the bottom side of art projects roasting away in the kiln. I pictured us in junior high school together, passing notes back and forth, stuffed into the part of a pencil sharpener that held the lead shavings.

I really hope my parents dont have
another baby. Theyve been spending alotta
time together lately + they keep giving us
outdoor chores. Gross!
  BFF Addie

Come to my house after school?
We can make choc chip b-bread.
I will protect you from procreation!!!
  BFF Leah

Best Friends Forever. Of course, her death eliminated the second F of that acronym. Probably for the better, anyway.

✂

Seamless panties. Ring tones. Corduroy. Used books. Tofurkey. Is it me, or have my simple pleasures gotten simpler?

✂

I am getting the hang of this church thing, the ritualistic standing and sitting and kneeling and shaking hands.

The businessman at the ... stand (podium? pulpit? lectern?) is clearly focused on something else during the reading. Equality becomes "equity," accountable becomes "accountantable."

I decline eating the body of Christ. I know what it's like to have everybody take a piece of you. I watch the swarm around me chew and chew, grind flesh between the grooves of their teeth.

2:27 Philippians
For indeed he was sick almost unto death; but God had mercy on him, and not only on him but on me also, lest I should have sorrow upon sorrow.

✂

It was only the one time, and it was before my diagnosis. He was sitting across from me on the C-train; he was already on when I got on, but I didn't notice him. He was slightly chubby — big boned, I suppose — and had a rounded look to his face that gave him a look of universal satisfaction. He wore long khaki shorts with a dusty appearance, as though covered with a fine layer of dirt. His legs, exposed at the knee, revealed hair the colour of pepper. A scar on his left leg ran from his ankle bone around to his Achilles tendon. He was wearing a cap so low on his head that I couldn't see what colour his hair was, or whether, for that matter, he had any. The brim of his cap had been bent into a broad curve, the same happy curve as his jawline.

After three stops, the recording that came on to announce the stops began to speed up. It announced Centre Street

Station like a chipmunk. He looked up. Even when he looked up, you still couldn't see what colour his hair was. He looked across at me, then up, as though glancing in the direction where he thought the voice might be coming from.

Then he asked if my name was Sabine, starting with, "I hope this doesn't sound creepy, but I think I know you."

✕

As a child, when Sabine would piss me off, I would go into my room and write her obituary. The year she turned eleven, she died in a house fire, fell off (and was trampled by) a horse, and accidentally ate some poisonous sushi. Once, she informed me, under her breath at a fancy dinner with our grandmother, that the lasagna I'd just eaten had *not*, in fact, been vegetarian, like she'd promised. That night, I made her kidnapped, at gunpoint, naturally, and nobody would pay her ransom.

Sometimes I wonder, pinpricks of karma climbing feather soft up my spine, is this why all the bad things happened to me?

✕

"Please keep the sick and dying in your prayers. Jenny Stratton. Olga Stamninski. Peter Craig. Samuel Mennit. Josie Feedler-Wayburn."

✕

My father had a partial set of false teeth, a wire retainer on whose bottom left side two gleaming white nubs were affixed. When he wore the device, you could barely tell they were fake. Outside of his mouth, however, overtly set beside his dinner plate, wet and shiny with his saliva, they looked more like the pieces of corn I'd painted with whiteout and placed under my pillow in hopes of gaining quarters. Crude, and counterfeit. Sometimes I'd wondered if other people were 100 percent natural, scanning for glass eyes and peg legs, clip-on hair extensions.

When my dad was a kid, those particular teeth grew in crookedly, forced up against each other to the point where both bent out awkwardly in a diagonal v-shape. They eventually became rotten, hollowed out on the inside. Before my dad finally got braces in junior high, his dentist had pulled the two adult teeth, ruling them unsalvageable.

(57

This is the image that comes to mind whenever someone asks me about my sister. Us growing up side by side, awkward and forced. There was no root canal. Just a slow, progressive rotting.

This is the image that comes to mind whenever someone asks me about my sister: My father's damaged smile.

✕

Sure enough, it does exist.

Mama Burns' Vegetarian Haggis

Ingredients

- 1/3 cup mashed dry kidney beans
- 2/3 cup diced carrots
- 1/4 tsp cayenne pepper
- 1 cup dry lentils
- 1/2 cup canned mushrooms
- 1 1/3 cup finely minced onion
- 1 1/2 tbsp soya sauce
- 1 tbsp rosemary
- 1 cup chicken broth
  (may substitute vegetable stock if desired)
- 1 large egg
- 1 tbsp lemon juice
- 1 1/4 tbsp vegetable oil
- 2 1/4 cups oats
- 2 tbsp ground peanuts (optional)
- 1 1/2 tsp thyme

Directions

Heat vegetable oil in saucepan, and sauté onion until tender, but not brown (3-5 minutes).
Mix in remaining vegetables and sauté another 5-7 minutes.
Stir in broth, lentils, kidney beans, peanuts, soya sauce, and lemon.
Season to taste with spices.
Bring to boil and reduce heat.
Allow to simmer (approximately 8 minutes).
Add oats, cover, and simmer on low.
Stir egg into saucepan and transfer mixture into a 6" x 8" greased baking tin.
Bake at 385° F for approximately 25-30 minutes, until toothpick comes out clean.

I pin my cellphone between my shoulder and my cheek; the heat of the battery stings my skin pink. "Hey, Dad, want to come over for dinner? I found a good recipe."

⋉

We got off simultaneously at Victoria Park, my ball capped stranger and I. Only he wasn't a stranger. Like I said, it was before my diagnosis. So I have no excuse.

Our simultaneous rising from our seats as the train hiccupped to a stop had caused me to lose my balance, my hands unthinkingly thrust outwards towards him for stability.

"No," I said, "You're thinking of my sister. I'm Leah; I was a couple of years behind her in school."

"Right!" I'd figured out who he was now, memory slowly tickling across my brain the way your foot regains feeling after falling asleep. He was the son of some friends of our parents, who adopted him at age three from a co-worker with a coke habit. What they had always called fate when describing his adoption story, he himself had always considered his nemesis. His name? Jack. Their last name? Jackson. Around him, Sabine had always referred to herself as Sabine Sabineson. But despite Bean's blatant mockery of his moniker, I'd once flipped through his sketchbook when he wasn't looking and discovered several caricatures of her. Suited up for a swim meet, a jump rope wielded above her head, asleep in the hammock stretched between our backyard trees. All with the same single feature overemphasized, out of proportion: her mouth.

He asked me how she was.

"Okay," I said, and then, "You work down here?" an innocent change of subject.

"No. I'm picking up my friend's car. I'm going on a business trip to Red Deer for the weekend."

"What do you do?" I wanted him to say artist. Put the name Jack Jackson and those massive lips to good use. I wanted us to have something in common. We stopped at the edge of the crosswalk. He rolled upwards on the balls of his feet, a rocking motion, a cannot-be-still motion.

"I'm in research." He glanced over at me as the light changed, a posed smile, his lips open only slightly, like the

stiff shell of a pistachio. "I'm going to Red Deer for a conference, I just have to pick up a buddy's car for the drive up.
I'm sorry I thought you were your sister. It's just … you look
freakishly alike."

"Yeah?" I said, "What is it? Eyes? Hair? Mouth?"

"I'm not too sure," he said, and his smile broke loose,
unprotected.

✂

3:16 Revelations
**But because you are lukewarm, neither hot nor cold, I am
going to spit you out of my mouth.**

✂

A guy came to my junior high once, Christopher something,
who was in a car accident, suffered injuries I can't recall
in detail other than a shattered windshield, pieces of glass
imbedded in his body. He lived, but in an amputated, wheelchair bound, slightly brain damaged state, preaching about
seatbelt safety. "It takes one second to do up your seat belt, but
you could be paralyzed for the rest of your life." It reminded
me of the condom commercials they'd begun showing us in
Health. By the time I reached high school, however, I saw on
the news that Christopher had died of a completely unrelated
case of MS, undetected until after his accident, once he was
in the care of a swarm of doctors, puppet to a host of medical
tests. I picture them checking and poking and prodding while
Christopher, feverish with advocacy, campaigns through his
twitches. To kill him so fast, the MS must have been a pretty
bad case.

I can't tell you how many times I've heard "What doesn't
kill you makes you stronger," or "God never gives us more
than we can handle." Is all that true, or is it made up by
those who are afraid of the possibility that it isn't true?
Because it seems, at least for Christopher, that he handled
what was given to him better than whatever forces out there
could have anticipated. So they tried another tactic, got him
that way.

✕

Hers is the voice that says, "Try the cortisone cream first, and call me if it doesn't clear up."

"But isn't skin one of the common spots that breast cancer spreads to?" My disease is in remission, but not my thoughts. Paranoia multiplies and spreads the same way cancer does.

She sighs. "There are links, yes, but it could also just be a rash."

"It's red," I say. "It's rough. It's itchy, it's scaly, and it's more inflamed than it was a week ago."

"Leah, I know, it's a good thing you know what to look for and you're keeping an eye out. I just don't think we need to panic every time —"

"*You* don't need to panic every time," I say, "*I*, however, I need to panic every time."

She holds a prescription out for me. "Try the cortisone. If it hasn't cleared up within a week, you can make another appointment."

I imagine myself chained to the exam table, wearing a T-shirt reading, "Be Your Own Advocate," ranting about patient rights. Around me, women missing their breasts wave posters in the air, pictures of rashes, of lumps, of gnarled tumours clawing at their brain stems.

In ancient Greek mythology, Amazon women were said to cut or burn off one breast in order to harvest and divert its strength, to better enable themselves to carry a bow and arrow. These warrior women lived independently, mating briefly with men in the neighbouring tribes, killing any resulting male offspring. Some think that the word Amazon itself (as I learned in my early university career, those half-course equivalents in Poli Sci, Anthropology, Greek and Roman Studies) means "no breast." *Amazon: derived from the preface "a-" meaning "without" and "mazos" meaning "breast."*

I take the prescription from her outstretched hand. (61

✕

Oedipus, mollusk, loofa, pomegranate.

✂

About the same time I got cancer, my sister began her second degree, this time in English, a radical departure from her Bachelor's in Kinesiology. The change surprised me, though it shouldn't have. As kids, Bean was always obsessed with words, loved to catch people's mispronunciations. She herself over-articulated every ambiguously syllabic word, preferring three syllables to two. In her own name, the German "e" at the end was its own syllable, the same "ah" sound at the end of my name. Sa-bee-nah. But people always pronounced hers wrong, dropping the "e" altogether, making Sabine so frustrated that she would gnaw on her own fingers. "Not prob-lee," she'd insist, "Prob-a-bly. Not Porsh, Por-schaaa." She had funny phonetic cues to help her remember how to spell words, of which I can only remember Mary-Jew-Anna (marijuana) and fuck-see-ah (fuchsia). Fuchsia was the colour of her bedroom.

I heard of her plans through a cousin who came to visit me early on during my hospitalization, not because the cousin told me, but because I'd asked. Back then, I was keeping pretty good tabs on her.

✂

"Jenny Stratton. Olga Stamninski. Peter Craig. Samuel Mennit. Josie Feedler-Wayburn."

✂

My friend Amanda wants to memorialize her pregnancy belly, before the birth, before she's too fat to want to engage in any activity.

"I'm going to be overdue," she says. "My mom says it runs in my family. She was two weeks overdue with me, and my grandma was a month overdue with my uncle; that was back when you didn't induce, and my uncle was born twelve pounds and had two teeth."

I wonder why I can't smell the fresh orange paint of the nursery they completed yesterday. A side effect I don't know about?

Amanda gathers her girlfriends, asks us to join her in the construction of a belly cast. I can't help but stare at her domed stomach, the way her belly button has popped. She is Woman, new and improved, tri-breasted. She has boobs worthy of commemoration, boobs to spare. We dip strips of plaster into buckets of water, spread the pieces across her dome while she squeals against the slap of cold.

"Remember doing this in art class?" she asks me. I can feel a soft undulation under where I am laying the plaster. A heel. "And you ..." She waits for me to finish. In art class in high school, where we first met, we teamed up to construct masks on other's faces. When the plaster dried on mine, it tore at my hairline, at my eyebrows. She'd forgotten to use Vaseline.

Amanda painted hers like a yin-yang. I painted mine the colour of flesh, made pink into the same thin lips and spherical cheeks that would hide behind it.

✕

Time simultaneously becomes longer and shorter. Longer, as in, the length of time between each of my checkups; shorter, as in the duration of time each checkup lasts. You'd think this would be a good sign.

✕

At fifteen, I sponge painted the walls of my new bedroom at my dad's, while Eightball weaved in and out between the cans of sapphire and cherry and cobalt, lifting his paws and giving the cans a perplexed look. I pictured Sabine telling me, "This is where the word *pussyfoot* comes from." I sponged red in the corner by the door, slowly changing colours until the dye morphed into a pallid blue.

Years later, that pattern of blues and reds is how I reacted to being told I had cancer. Panic so strong it knocked the wind out of me. The colour of a scream.

✕

"Please keep the sick and dying in your prayers. Jenny Stratton. Peter Craig. Samuel Mennit. Josie Feedler-Wayburn. The rose of welcome for newborns is for —"

On Sunday, Olga Stamninski isn't on the list anymore.

✕

Here's the thing — I went with him, Jack Jackson, to Red Deer that day.

We didn't drive together, couldn't possibly, as he was stay-ing for his conference. We got his friend's car first, and he drove me home to get mine. He slowed and rolled through a stop sign, steered the car right with one hand while fumbling with a cassette tape. "You take a right on which street again?" He had a red butterfly cut-out dangling from the rearview mirror; it reeked of citrus, the fake air freshener scent of the tropics. He pulled up in front of my condo.

I got out and started my car. Justin's car. Our car. My car. I can't remember what we were calling it then.

I followed him down Deerfoot and onto Highway 2. He left his cap on in the car, and drove in the slow lane.

I couldn't remember what colour his hair was.

✕

When I was fifteen, I figured that had she lived, Adelaide would have probably gotten pregnant. She was, I assumed, the type to rebel. Her family, which would have grown by three more chil-dren by then, would be unsupportive and kick her out, and she would come live with me in my father's basement, shaded from the spring heat that led to her May due date. We would lounge in patio furniture dragged in from outside, eating hummus spread generously on salted crackers, our bare toes dangling on the cement floor. My imagination held Adelaide in a bathing suit, a one piece, blue fabric stretched sheer and glossy over her expanding belly. The baby would have masses of black hair, which would fall out, and grow back in blond.

We would take feeding shifts during the night, and then, during the day, still too young to work or drive, take the C-train downtown, swapping the baby's sling whenever our backs got tired. We would wander the booths at the Lilac festival in flip-flop sandals, and Addie would break a piece of the purple blossoms off a tree and tuck them behind the baby's ear. We would unpack our lukewarm juice boxes and sit next to the river while the baby slept, nocturnal, bur-rowed heat in the hollow of my crossed legs.

We would both have long hair.

✕

Kumquat, billy goat, smorgasbord, spatula.

⊱

There is one memory, although bits of it escape me. My mother and sister were there, and I remember the tangerine and mint coloured checkerboard of the mall floor, but not what we were shopping for. I remember that Bean and I were both still organically blond.

We were approached outside of a cinnamon bun kiosk, although this detail may or may not be accurate, because other memories of the mall (mostly from my teens) do not include it. I remember it was a man who approached us, but thinking back, there's a possibility he was only a teenager. I was still young enough to think that anyone as big as my parents was a grown-up. He had flowers, but they were wrapped so you couldn't see what kind they were.

"Hey, could I ask you guys a favour? See that girl behind the counter?" He pointed into a store. Her hair was an unnatural ginger colour, coily, and pinned back. "I want to ask her out, but I want to surprise her." He was speaking to Bean and me. "Do you think you two could just bring those in there for her? Don't tell her who they're from, though. There's a card; she'll see it. You'd just have to drop them off really quick."

My mother answered, as though he'd been asking her, though in retrospect, he probably should have. We had a lot of shopping left to do, she explained, and I remember wondering why she was so curt.

"Mom," Bean asked, once we were out of earshot, "why are you such a spoilsport?"

"Don't get involved in other people's business," she replied.

⊱

A reporter calls me, asks to write our story. Says she heard about me through a friend, a nurse at Foothills when I was an inpatient.

"Isn't that illegal?" I ask, "Aren't there like, confidentiality waivers nurses have to sign?"

"Of *course* there are!" she says, "This is the opposite of violating your rights. We'd like to see that you're recognized for your heroism. You, and your boyfriend. I'm working on

(65

a piece about incredible love stories, and I think whenever
a couple experiences something traumatic —"

I interrupt her, "Listen, I don't think I can help you. We're
not together anymore. So ..." There is a pause on the other
end. I am going to be late for work. "You can interview me,
if you want. Since you've already violated my constitutional
right to privacy."

"Well," she says, and then again, "well, I really just need
couples."

✂

Salamander, urethra, baboon, goulash, oy.

✂

In my new one-bedroom basement suite, I have trouble falling
asleep. Restless and shifting, I try to picture the condo. I open
the door, applying pressure to the damaged handle before
twisting it left and pulling it back. I follow the carpeted stairs
to the halfway point, where they fork off, marked by a small
countertop braced between the right angle of the wall. The
doorbell rings. I turn around to see who it is.

✂

Dear Leah,
It is TOTALLY 100% unfair that Bean always
gets her way. I don't know why you're MOM
favers her because you are so much the
better daughter. Your sister should get a life.
I cant wait until we are grownups and can
move out of our parents houses. I cant wait
to get away from everybody and finelly
have my own room and privacy!!! I know we
both have it pretty sucky right now but I
know someday we will have perfect lives
and really really hot husbands and a normal
amount of kids. And we will love them all equal.
It will all be worth it in the long run.

Pinky swear
     BFF Addie

✂

It begins to snow around four o'clock, thick, asymmetrical flakes like Tetris pieces, loosely packed with gaps in between. It accumulates quickly — by five it covers my basement window, the way I played Tetris as a child, giving up when things got tough, rotating the pieces into shapes that no longer fit until they'd reached the top of the screen.

I drive over to the condo, watching the shadows of the street lights dive in front of me, committing suicide by jumping into my path.

✂

breast brest *n.* **1** either of two milk-secreting glandular organs on the chest of a woman. **2** the seat of affection and emotion: "Griefs of mine own lie heavy in my breast" (Shakespeare).

✂

I am sick of the pink ribbons. Slap a pink ribbon on stationery, stuffed poodles, bracelets, toques, car windshields, lapels. Silly, smiling women walking for a cure, shouting empowerment in the air, clutching their mothers and daughters to their chests. They think the pink ribbons are points — collect enough and breast cancer will disappear. They don't understand. This game has endless levels. You can play as long as you want.

✂

I don't know exactly what my sister looks like now, but I know what she looked like then. I see her sometimes before I drift off to sleep, wet and shiny in her black one-piece, standing by the edge of the pool, the thick straps marking deep indents in her freckled shoulders. She would have outgrown a suit a year. I can see the bulge of ponytail tucked into her swim cap, hair she refused to cut even when the other girls on the team forfeited their own locks to be more aerodynamic. She said looking like a guy would slow down her social life more than it would speed up her breast stroke.

✂

There are still foods that elicit curls of queasiness in my stomach basin, foods that, in the beginning, I ate just before chemo, not realizing the associations I was setting up for myself. Biology kicked in, ruining my fondness for soft cheeses, for dark carbonated beverages, for the sizzling chunky tomato sauce I routinely poured over pasta.

This was, perhaps, for the time being, biology's only triumph, my normal bodily processes having fallen victim to whatever consequences chemo could think of. Chemo sprouted acne along my hair and lip lines, corroded my gums. Chemo ignored my fibre intake and crowded my bowels, looked away when I woke up hot and wet with night sweats, even as I peeled sticky sheets away from myself at two, three, four o'clock in the morning.

Not that the clockwork of my body didn't eventually win back some points, budding hair on my rashy scalp that was thicker and paler than before, holding tighter to the fodder in my belly, refusing to let it rocket back up. But it hasn't been *fully* itself since.

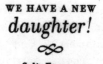

WE HAVE A NEW
daughter!

∞

Solie Frances
November 5, 2005
3:13 AM
11 lbs 2 oz
22.7 inches

*In the depths of winter,
I finally learned that
within me there lay an
invincible summer.*

Amanda and Kenneth

✂

Our first Halloween together, Justin and I went as Hansel and Gretel. The second year we were salt and pepper shakers.

As children, my sister and I often dressed up for Halloween together too. There are pictures of me, as an infant, dressed as a caterpillar, Bean in a sparkling blue (but Kool-Aid stained) gymnastics leotard and wings my mother had made from stretching navy nylons around clothes hangers.

When I was eight, we fashioned our own juvenile versions of pencil (her) and eraser (me). Then, that night at dinner, she threw up dead cow burgers all over the kitchen floor. I was forced to go out without her, an anonymous, ill-shaped pink blob. Without her, nobody knew what I was.

✂

Jack Jackson.

He and I were already there, had pulled off the highway onto Red Deer's main strip of restaurants, alongside a Petro Canada. We'd stopped here often on family trips, but I'd never driven it myself.

I watched him step out of his car, stretch, beckon towards me, lift a pump off the self-serve.

✂

I ring the doorbell to the condo, shaking snow out of the folds of my parka, and Justin answers while in mid-ramble, the phone trapped between his ear and shoulder. He says, to the phone, "I'll have to call you back," and then, to me, in an tone that is both awkward and relieved, "Hey, Lee." Pretending he expected this.

"Hey," I say.

"Hey," he says again. "I like your ponytail."

)(four

What I've said hasn't been the *whole* truth.

But it's been what you wanted to hear.

⨉

Another funny word. Sabotage.

⨉

One pair of panties.

One pair of thick strapped, full-back, red-bordered pink panties, sprinkled with polka dots in various sizes as though paint splattered. The price tag was still attached. They weren't even that expensive.

"You girls think you can just take things without paying for them?" The mall security guard had refused to touch the panties since he positioned them on the table in front of us. Four ninety-nine, the tag told me.

"I had nothing to do with it," I said, again. "Take our mother's number, go ahead."

When he left us alone, behind the heavy door, Sabine said, "I've done it before, you know. It's not that big of a deal."

"Just shut up," I said. "Just stop talking. What the hell is wrong with you? You're going to go to jail for a pair of underwear. You're going to be banned from the mall. Good going, idiot. Mom and Dad are going to kill you. And don't even try telling them I had anything to do with it. As it is, I'm never speaking to you again."

"I did it before," she repeated. "I just never got caught. You're just bad luck."

⨉

I didn't stay in Red Deer, because it was the first time, and I hadn't learned yet. What I could and couldn't do, which is different than what I should and shouldn't do.

I drove home without the radio on, in a single quickest-route path, leaving the windows rolled up as the day's temperature increased, slowly turning the car into a sauna, sweat making my skin itch. The Almost of what happened making me want to scratch.

I pictured what would have happened if I had gotten out of my car instead of turning around and driving out of the parking lot. I saw us ordering fries but not eating them. Getting a hotel room, lying down in the bed, but fully clothed. I saw myself taking his cap off, but this scene always finished before I saw the colour of his hair.

Since learning what I can and can't do, I've played the scene again. Left his cap on, let him undress me. I would have asked him if he'd ever sketched me.

"Now that I see you up close," he would say, "you actually do look quite different. And she had a birthmark right here," and he would place his palm over my belly button and touch his index finger to the ridge of my lowest rib.

But this scene stops too, pauses when I remember I had two breasts then. The breasts in my mind would have burst out of my 34.B bras, two flashy full moons. I let him fully expose them, nipples 'n' all. I let the me in this scene raise her arms sexily above my head, watch the breasts raise and flex in tandem, as though inhaling. We all hold our breath.

><

The morning I was told I had cancer, we fell back asleep, and my wet hair dried cold against Justin's shoulder. When I woke up, he had a clump of green discharge in the crook of his eye.

My tumour, sickle shaped and hard, like a cashew, muttered, "Gross!"

I watched the glob, watched it grow larger. Watched the fractured lines of dry skin across his elbows, slid my body away from the latent clutch of his hands, his fingers curled like he was holding something, even in his sleep. Holding, perhaps, breasts.

My tumour, sickle shaped and hard, like a cashew, muttered, "I'm gonna be sick!"

And I thought, I will never have to worry about work or my family or Justin again.

><

My mother lives in the Maritimes, hating men. She has joined
a red hat club, and is learning French, or so her letters say,
challenging the ladies in her group to see who can compre-
hend the most. "Tout le monde portant une jupe jaune, prenez
un dollar de la fiole." I picture my mother getting dressed for
French class, pulling a skirt over her leggings, socks over her
nylons, earrings, bangle bracelets, a digital watch, an analog
watch. A belt, a sash. She is multi-outfitted, multi-hued. She
likes this game, she will win this game, and she will learn
French and pay her bills doing it. Her red hat will keep all the
masculine articles and verbs away.
><

Justin insists, "Don't let this be like last time, okay?" His hair
has dried lopsided, angled towel ruffled spikes pressed flat
on one side. He leans against the kitchen cupboard, a drawer
handle jutting into the small of his back. He shifts against it,
changing pose, reaching behind himself for the rim of the
counter as though bracing himself.

"Last ... last time I drove over to your house in hazardous
weather so that we could?..." Something grinds beneath my
foot, like sand along the tiled floor. Neither one of us enjoyed
the actual process of condo maintenance, high-fiving for
summer rain that watered the lawn for us, straightening
rather than filing increasing stacks of bills. But under the care
of only one haphazard, half-assed tidier, this home we called
ours has fallen into disarray. A bowl in the sink is ringed with
the pinkish bubbles of rinsed meat.

Justin asks, "So that we could?... Talk? Get back together?
What?"
><

Jack Jackson was the first, when I decide to count him. With
the second, I learned not to leave enough time to talk myself
out of it.

This was at a friend's party, the summer before I was diagnosed. Justin was with a friend, at a concert I'd opted out of. I
went upstairs with the cousin of my friend, the host. At least it
was safe. There were balloons filled with Curacao and vodka;

upstairs in what was likely the guest bedroom, he squished a
purple one in his hand but it bulged through his fingers and
squirmed away from him, bounced to the floor. The liquid,
blue-black behind the stretched indigo rubber, settled to the
bottom of the balloon, relieved.

I undressed myself, shucking off my jeans, twisting myself
out of the bra whose straps I'd hooked into an x across my
back. When I say I undressed myself, I mean I did so fully, not
engaging in the kind of cross-body fumbling typical of hurried first-time liaisons.

I should have realized it was all the same, exactly like
the cheating I'd done before. Violation of intimacy, of trust,
of commitment. Extramarital. Extra-relational. Extra-
familial.

Lacking loyalty.

I never told Justin, making me wonder why I did it in the
first place.

One thing I know I'm good at. Being the right person to the
wrong person at the wrong time.

≍

What *didn't* start a fight with Bean and me?

How I hated it when she dangled her hand off the top
bunk when going to sleep, her creepy, dead-body arm keeping me awake.

How she told me I could make special health-food
Dunkaroos by dipping Flintstone vitamins into bubblegum
flavoured toothpaste.

How she plucked all her eyelashes out in an attempt to
accumulate enough wishes to get Chad MacDonald to go out
with her (Mom had told us that if you found an eyelash, you
were supposed to blow it away and make a wish).

How I tattled on her after catching her prank-calling the
Children's Help Phone. "I think my dad is cheating on my
mom," she was saying. "I don't know if I'm supposed to tell
anyone." Another thing she never got in trouble for.

After our fights, Bean and Mom would go for private walks
around the neighbourhood. Sometimes this was after dark. I
was never allowed to go. I always figured it was to keep the two

of us apart, but I preferred to stay home anyway. We had an off-white couch on which Chief had thrown up once, leaving a large russet discolouration. I would perch on that cushion, flipped over of course, and watch *The Muppet Show* with my dad. I figured it was lucky.

In the hospital, I wondered whether or not we would still fight if and when she came to visit. I knew she knew. Would my cancer make our animosity invalid? I didn't know the rules.

I pictured her and my mother, their matching high fore-heads and widow's peak hairlines, circling the block. Their matching blameless laughter.

⚞

It was my fault.

At some point, I stopped riding the C-train back and forth and put up posters at my dad's, making the spare room into a bedroom. At Dad's I was allowed to buy expensive, glamorous vegetarian alternatives (Nayonaise, RiceDream, Chinese no-meat balls), and own a kitten (85 percent black). Only later did I learn that a black cat was only bad luck if you came across it in the street. A black cat in the house was just the opposite.

My mother came to the hospital from the Maritimes only twice; both times she pulled a chair up to the left corner of my bed. I ignored her while she shifted it to her liking.

"They say your prognosis is very good," she told me, as though she didn't know they were telling me this bullshit too.

She came at good times for confirming her beliefs about me as a child, came when I was irritable and petulant, my skin bloated and retaining water, my fingers raw-pink and swollen, my distended legs barbed with thick fuzz, bristly as Justin's five o'clock shadow.

I remember that I was bitching about how gross it felt and that I was too insensate to be surprised when she volunteered.

She shaved my legs like she peeled potatoes, in long con-nected strips, periodically wetting the blade with a facecloth.

"Your sister called off the wedding," she said, as though I knew exactly what she was referring to. "She's always been like that."

"Like what?"

"She just … she knows exactly what she wants. She always has. I remember when she was especially small, she had a specific *way* of putting her shoes on. Left foot first, then right foot. Your father went to put them on once, and he did them backwards. And she leaned over and bit him right on the leg. He had a bruised ring of teeth marks on his calf for the whole rest of that week."

"And that's supposed to be a good thing?"

"Sometimes. Our best attributes are our worst downfalls."

"Okay," I said, giving up.

She slid the razor delicately over an imperceptible patch of remaining stubble on the bridge of my knee.

"You, on the other hand, you were always so *easy*."

When she left my room, she put a tub of cold cream on my dinner tray. "I use this for the dark circles under my eyes. I mean, you can use it anywhere, but it seems to help inflammation."

I unscrewed the lid. One of her eyelashes was stuck in the cream. I took the eyelash out and held it, blew to make a wish. The eyelash stayed in place, pasted to the edge of my finger.

✕

Only weeks after I am discharged, Justin doesn't come home from work. Given that my boredom has been channelled into reality TV, I don't notice his absence until my cellphone vibrates off the coffee table and I realize I've fallen asleep on the couch, a headache growing behind the glasses I have neglected to remove.

"I have bad news," he informs me, and then, "Were you sleeping? Are you okay? You're not feeling sick, are you?" His own voice is thick with mucous, and he sniffs deeply, snot gurgling in his nasal cavities. "I started feeling like shit over lunch-time, and now I can barely breathe. So the thing is, I don't think I should come home tonight, because your immune system is still crappy."

"Okay," I say. "Yeah. You're probably right."

"Do you want me to call your dad?" he suggests, "Just so

you're not completely alone? I don't like the idea of you being alone."

"I'm a big girl," I say. "You sound like you need someone to take care of *you*, though."

"Someone to play nurse, maybe?" he jokes. He is losing his voice. "I think I'm going to crash at Steve's," he whispers.

"What?"

"Crash. At. Steve's ... on his couch." He pauses, sniffs. "Can I at least let your dad know? Just in case something happens?"

"I'll call him," I say. "Feel better though, okay?"

"I miss you," he says. His m comes out like a b. *I biss you.*

I have never really preferred joint sleeping arrangements, finding the solid spread of my own flung limbs and pillow drool more restful than the fidgety sleep we frequent together, his face-down fumbling for my waist, the dart of his leg as my feet brush cold up against it.

I go directly from the couch to my bed and sleep soundly, unbroken. My dreams gush and spill vivid pictures across the panorama of my brain. I sleep through the shudder-ing ring of my phone as he calls to make sure I haven't felt poorly, or missed him, or died in my sleep.

We have not gotten used to each other after all.

✕

As a little girl, I always questioned the last thing that was said at sleepover parties before everybody fell asleep, twelve-year-olds used to having their own bedrooms, tongues bruised garish blue-black from wildberry Skittles. Were you supposed to say "Good night?" or were you allowed to let eyelids drop on discussions over who had cramps and who had outgrown their AA cups?

I am wide awake, having, after four-ish months of being apart, driven over to Justin's in the middle of a storm, my speeding mind making up for the cautious slothfulness of the car on its way over, compacting snow into perfect path-ways, laboriously straight.

To Justin, in tousled sheets that aren't mine stretched over a bed that once was, I say, "I think a lady at the church

I started going to died. They had her name on the prayers for the sick list for weeks, and then one day she was gone."

"Maybe she got better?" Justin suggests, sneezes, his voice unusually nasal. I wonder if he thought about calling me to take care of him when he got sick. "It's equally likely she got better, like you did. Have you seen an obituary?" Then, "Listen, do you hear that? The neighbour keeps letting his new dog out in the middle of the night, and I can swear, I can hear it licking itself."

✕

Of those who were the last to speak with my mother before May sixth — and I was not one of them — two, including my sister, remember that her voice disappeared as though cut off, every two minutes or so. The hallmark of a cellphone running out of batteries.

When neither Bean nor I could get a hold of her for three days, my father filed a missing person's report, and was told there was nothing he could do. She was a grown woman, unmarried, living alone. Her children were no longer at home.

"She would never, *ever*, stop talking to her daughters," my dad insisted, his words a lie only Sabine believed. "This is completely out of character."

Only when we were informed that she hadn't been at work the last two days were we able to proceed with the paperwork.

When she finally contacted us the following day from a 506 area code, she told me this was her life's calling. She had to go. The fact that her desire to escape was so strong, she couldn't ignore it. It was a sign.

Those were her words. Mine were that I would never understand.

All my life, all I'd wanted my mother to have was faith.

As though one can just *have* faith, as one *has* a bowl of Cheerios.

✕

Serenaded by the dog still licking itself outside, I peel myself away from Justin's sleeping torso and slip into the condo's only bathroom to run myself a bath. Snow is stacked against the windows, thick with cold condensation. I trace a figure eight into the fog, a vertical infinity. Sideways it can go on forever; this way it is that much less.

The medicine cabinet we shared just months ago is empty of my powder blush and ratio base lotion, my compilation of bobby pins, but still, the bathroom seems to remember me. I lower myself into the tub and sink to my knees, a line bisecting me at my bellybutton, boiled skin from pale.

I don't notice the blood until I see it in the water and touch my face reflexively. It comes thick from my nose, almost black, but turns red when it slips through my fingers and hits the water, hangs suspended in clots, swirls symmetrically outwards like a Rorschach.

✂

As the only one of my friends without a full-time job, when Kenneth is in the field and Amanda feels "fluish," I am the one she calls.

She answers the door in one of Kenneth's undershirts, the thin white cotton stained clear with breast milk, making visible the pinched flesh of nipple beneath. Her jeans are unzipped, the hem of her shirt unevenly tucked in. Her face is flushed.

"I don't even feel like a human, like a woman," she confesses later, nursing completely topless in front of me, Solie's bare body like an appendage, an asexual look-alike budding from Amanda's breast. Life sprouts from Amanda's body, takes up independent existence. "I haven't had a haircut in months," Amanda is saying, "I'm just globs of excess fat. My breasts are like balloons. I thought all the excess body hair I had when I was pregnant would go away after the birth, but I'm like, an animal. She hangs off me like a koala or something." She sticks her finger between Solie's lips to break the suction. "Sweet Jesus. Do you know how much this hurts?"

✂

"This mass is for the repose of the soul of Olga Stamninski."

)(five

2 years, 9 months, 1 week, 1 day.

   1,012 days total.

   Approximately 144 weeks

   or 24,288 hours

   or 1,457,280 minutes

   or 87,436,800 seconds.

   Our first go-round, in its entirety, from our first day as a couple to our last day in Penticton.

   3 months, 23 days.

   115 days total.

   2760 hours

   165,600 minutes

   9,936,000 seconds, from our last day in Penticton to the day I walked outside and swept the snow off the front windshield of my car with sopping mittened hands, waited in the frozen belly of the vehicle while the motor reluctantly groused into gear, and then drove over to Justin's, knowing the whole time that I shouldn't. Give or take.

   Do you start counting again if you don't see there being an end?

✂

I run into my anesthesiologist while trying on jeans, jeans that sit awkwardly on my frame now, forced wide by the jutting hip bones I inherited from my mother, but gaping pouches in the front and back where skin and fat have sublimated. Coming out of the change room, pulling the drawstring of my sweatpants tight, I see her once, and by habit I see her face in its inverse, the image of her at the head of the operating table leaning over me, a surgical mask, then eyes, eyebrows, hairline. Separate from the words I hear but don't see. She closes in, covers my mouth. *Count backwards from ten.*

   "That woman was my anesthesiologist," I tell Amanda, waiting on a couch just outside the change room.

She is on her cellphone, and waves at me to hush. "The sitter says Solie has the hiccups," she says, when she hangs up. "What were you saying? Who was?..."

"My anesthesiologist," I say, and turn, but she has left the store.

She looks disappointed. "Oh. Really? You remember what she looked like? Wouldn't you have only seen her, like, once? And been passing out at the time?" She laughs at this.

"It was a memorable moment," I say. "And it wasn't that long ago."

"It was *ages* ago!" she says. "I've had a kid in between." She smiles at me, "You know, you don't have to hold onto those memories anymore. You're not going to die, okay? Really. It's not going to happen. Okay? It's *not* going to happen."

✂

Father Siddons catches me off guard one Sunday after the service. I've always been tempted to slip out after communion, but I don't know the rules. In a religion I don't even belong to, I stand and sit and kneel with everyone else while the processional music finally drains, five verses and a repeated chorus later, long after the priest has pulled his robe over his head and started hand shaking in the hall. Families line up beside me to get donuts, a rare and ironic treat in a business so poor it has to collect handouts. Father Siddons's lips are powder white; his stomach bulges behind his plain cotton T-shirt. Having taken off his robe, he looks like the rest of the throng. His eyes are blotchy up close, accented with puffy bruises in the shape of half moons. His hand brushes my arm, a hand so big it is almost a paw. I am surprised at both the being touched and the gentleness of it, how something so cumbersome can hold so delicately.

"I'm sorry," he says. "We've never really met formally. I've noticed you here before, though, and I saw you the other afternoon at the Foothills Hospital while I was, you know, visiting some parishioners that are, well, have taken ill. I wanted to come over and say hello but I was sort of tied up in a conversation, and so, well, I just wanted to make sure you knew it wasn't intentional. I didn't want to seem rude."

"Oh," I say, and then, a repeating chorus, "Oh, um, no, that's okay. I was visiting someone ill too."

I suppose lying within holy walls is against the rules.

✂

STAMNINSKY, Olga.
1921–2005

It is with great sorrow that we mourn the passing of our mother and sister, Olga, at the age of 84 after a lengthy and courageous battle with breast cancer. Olga was born in Leader, Saskatchewan, in 1921, and came to Calgary, Alberta, with her parents, John and Evelyn, when she was only four years old. After completing her schooling, Olga became a teacher and spent many years in a profession she loved. Olga was a devout Catholic and committed many volunteer hours to her church. She will be greatly missed by her sister, Corinne Rosenberg (Harold), six nieces, and four nephews. Donations in Olga's memory can be made to the Tom Baker Cancer Centre in Calgary, Alberta.

PART A –
EMPLOYEE LOCATION TRANSFER APPLICATION

NOTE: The contractual obligations of employment specify that employees may transfer at their own request, but will otherwise be asked to remain in the location and position for which they were originally hired.

All location transfers represent requests initiated by the employee.

03/01/2006	252 359	HUMAN RESOURCES
DATE OF REQUEST (DD/MM/YYYY)	JOB REQ. NO*	HIRING DEPARTMENT*

APPLICANT INFORMATION –

JORDAN, LEAH I.

NAME (LAST/FIRST/MIDDLE INITIAL)

Applicant has been employed for probationary
period of at least 1 year: (yes) / no

Performance evaluation satisfactory or better: (yes) / no

EMPLOYMENT RECORD –

ACADEMIC SUPERVISOR	HR	E. STONE	$15/hr
PRESENT JOB TITLE	DEPARTMENT	SUPERVISOR	SALARY
01/02/2006	4671031	011684478	
START DATE (DD/MM/YYYY)	JOB TITLE CODE	EMPLOYEE NUMBER	

May the hiring department contact your current supervisor? (yes) / no

REASON FOR REQUEST:

RELOCATING OUT OF THE CITY

CURRENT LOCATION OF EMPLOYMENT   CALGARY, AB

PREFERRED LOCATION OF EMPLOYMENT   EDMONTON, AB

I have worked at the preferred location of employment before: yes / (no)

My signature below certifies that all statements on this form are accurate to the best of my knowledge.

x *L L Jordan*   03/01/2006

APPLICANT'S SIGNATURE   DATE (DD/MM/YYYY)

Shortly before my parents' divorce, I was falling asleep in front of the heating vent in my room, listening to their warped voices bicker through the hot air. I remember one morning after a particularly hateful explosion that began over whether or not my mother should have to chaperone Sabine's swim team trip to Montana, and distorted into my mother ranting about how the single mom whose kids Bean and I babysat was a "filthy, immoral, SLUT." I could not stop yawning one morning in art class, my hands gluey with papier maché, lobbing it onto the engorged balloon in front of me. That year I was in third grade. We were making globes.

I remember my teacher pulling up a chair beside me and asking whether there was anything wrong, why was I crying, and was there anything wrong at home?

"Um," I said, baffled at first, before realizing, "Oh, no, I'm just tired. My eyes water when I yawn." With the newspaper and adhesive all over my hands, I hadn't been able to wipe my face. "Don't worry," I added, intent on her knowing that I was just fine, and that I was a good girl, "what's wrong at home doesn't make me cry anymore."

She squatted beside my desk. "Okay," she said. Her eyes were bright and wet like the dolphins I'd seen at the Vancouver Aquarium. "Hey," she said, then, "You know what? I have some things I need to do in the classroom over lunchtime. Would you like to stay and keep me company? We could eat our lunches in here. And we could talk about whatever you want. What do you say?"

I didn't want to hurt her feelings, but the idea of staying inside the classroom during lunch made my stomach cringe. I smiled at her and her dolphin eyes.

"Actually, I promised Andrea and Shannon I'd hold the other end of the jump rope for them. But thanks!"

✕

The day I went to dinner at Andrew's was the third time. A door in the back hallway connected my lower basement suite to his upper two-bedroom. He had recently put new laminate flooring in the kitchen, pale yellow squares that reminded me of hospital hallways. We drank non-alcoholic punch out of real glasses, he showed me (illegally) his student's essay, I showed him (immorally) my non-hospital giant retro lime green and pink checker bedspread with the swooping white half circles and fuzzy Muppet-skin marshmallow teenage pillows. This was the third time.

We undressed ourselves, him from the top down, stretching out the width of the loop of his tie, fumbling with buttons, pushing his jeans down over his hips. It was a Friday. A casual Friday. I undressed from the bottom up, unzipping the small zipper sewn into the side of my skirt, slipping off my nylons. I left my tank top on over my bra, aware of the way my fake appendage slid and shifted behind these insecure layers while his body slid and shifted on top of me. He didn't ask why.

"I don't generally do this kind of thing," I told him, afterwards. I had gotten used to the cold that permeated my apartment at night, but goosebumps had sprouted along his arms. He put his shirt back on and did up the buttons, beginning at the bottom, the same way Justin did them. "Button-up Shirts" Justin called them, whereas I'd always called them "Button Down." It was a debate Justin had won. "You always focus on the negative. Glass half empty. Button *Down*." I didn't talk to him for an hour after that.

"Hey," Andrew said, "It's okay. I know you don't generally do this kind of thing. But … you're single right now. I'm single right now. It happens."

I wondered if it had happened to him before. "You sure that punch didn't have alcohol in it?"

"I'm sure," he said. "I'll give you the recipe sometime. If I forget, just come upstairs and ask."

"Really?" I ask. I want to make sure he means this. "I can just … come upstairs? And be like, hey Andrew, let's make … punch."

He smiles, a little lopsided. "You really liked the punch that much, eh?"

✂

I tell Justin my company is transferring me. I do it at our favourite Mexican joint in Kensington. There are grains of curried yellow rice like maggots all over the floor. Justin has one in the corner of his lip, three stuck to the cuff of his shirt. Long-distance relationships never work.

"They can't do that, can they?" he asks, but breezy, more focused on the way his quesadilla is collapsing, purging tomatoes and piquant peppers.

"It's a compliment," I say. "They asked me first. They had an opening. It was … they offered it to me, if, if I wanted to, um, to take it." If I say *they* enough, will my company get the blame, even though I filled out the paperwork?

"If they want to compliment you, they should promote you," he says, attempting to spear a lump of shredded chicken. "Oh, Jesus, this, it's everywhere! Can't they?… Oh, here, can I, can I borrow your napkin?"

"Justin! I'm trying to —"

"I know. Okay, yeah, I'm listening. So, did you ask for a raise?"

"That wasn't what I meant. Look, they're transferring me, okay? It's the same job, just in a different division. The Edmonton department is a much better equipped, um, you know, facility."

"What do you care?" he teases. "You hate your job."

"Not all the time. It might be a good opportunity. A good, you know, a good change. I need a change."

"You need a change, okay, let's go away for the weekend? We'll stay in the Fantasyland Hotel, in the igloo room. We'll melt all the walls, it'll be so hot."

"Justin. I'm talking about *moving*."

He pauses. "Does your dad know?" The kernel falls from his lip. "I love the guacamole here. We should do Mexican at home more, huh? I bet we could figure out the recipe." The guacamole is smudged now, across the heel of his hand. He licks it off and grins.

"I'm going," I say. "I want to go. Okay? I know you can't, really, because of your job, and stuff, and that's fine, *maybe* the long distance will be worth it. It's a good opportunity for me. We can try."

His is the same voice that said, *"Are you kidding? What about your … your treatments? Your doctors? You can't just up and … Jesus, Leah."*

Now he concedes, "You know," with no hint of annoyance, "it could be fun, and it's not too far."

"Well," I say. "It is three hours. Three and a half. Worse in the winter."

"Okay," he says, grabs his napkin from his lap and puts it on the table. "If you really want to go that bad, I'll go too. Long distance never works, and I mean, come on. So, yeah, we can go. I gotta pee. I'll be back in a minute."

We can go.

I watch him lope across the restaurant, away from me, if only for a minute.

✕

Mr. O's Grade Six Class Party Punch

(invented by The Grade Sixers)

Serves 30

1. Put 5 bananas in a bowl and squish them up.
2. Add 3 cans of chunky pineapple including the juices.
3. Pour one jug of fresh orange juice (with extra pulp) into the mixture slowly, and stir so that the bananas mix in.
4. Stir in one can of concentrated grape juice and one can of concentrated cranberry juice.
5. Add 3 bottles of ginger ale and empty three ice cube trays into the bowl.
6. Stir with a very big spoon.
7. Add one to two cans of fake cherries (those ones without the pits in them).
8. Voila!

✕

After the divorce, whenever we went on long car rides, my dad invented a game he called Brainlinks, which he and I played obsessively on the weekends that he had us, on the highway between Calgary and Sylvan Lake, where we would camp when it was warm enough outside. "Okay, Leah. First thing that

comes to mind. Flower." These were all things he could see
outside the window, a convenient way to entertain his daughters, or perhaps himself, while keeping his eyes on the road.

"Pot."

"Tree."

"House."

"Cow."

"Boy."

"Stop it!" Sabine would screech, "That's not how the game
works! You're not even playing it right! You're just making
compound nouns!"

✂

Hers is the same voice that asks me to speak at a support
group again, this time for women diagnosed under thirty.
I think, there's enough of us now to form a group.

"I think it would be really good — for them *and* for you —
if you would just go, give them hope that people do go into
remission, that people can have a normal life afterwards.
That people *do* beat this. Just tell them what you've learned."

I don't say this out loud. Can I tell them I have learned
nothing?

The wisdom is that, for me, there was no wisdom.

Cancer got me twice, me as a woman diagnosed under
thirty, impressionable enough for earth-shattering, wisdom-
inducing life events. It let me live. But only so that I could go
back to the way it was.

✂

My bum is pressed against the wall, my legs stretched vertically
up its length, the one pose I've retained from a three-hour-long
session in yoga mindfulness meditation during my chemo.
This upturned world comforts me, reminds me of not my first,
but my second period. The first had been uneventful. Being
the athlete she was, preying mantis arms and legs thrashing
through the water, Sabine's entrance into womanhood was
only six months before mine, despite me being three years
younger. My first was old news. My second, however, caught me   (87
off guard, corkscrew cramps that wrenched me out of a dream,
sent me stumbling into the bathroom, where I hovered over the

toilet but couldn't quite throw up. Instead, I lay on the floor and arched my back, balancing my ankles on the roll of toilet paper protruding from the wall. Later, I asked my mother to please schedule me a hysterectomy.

Justin's head leans over mine, comes into view. He pulls the sides of his mouth outward and waggles his tongue at me.

"Stop it," I say, and exhale. *Mindfulness.*

That day, my mother scowled at me. "Count your blessings," she informed me. "Those that experience pain in their youth will experience pleasure in their adulthood. It's karma."

"That was enough pain," I retorted. "I think I've earned no more school, peanut butter hazelnut toast served to me on a silver platter, and the abolition of all animal slaughterhouses."

I remember her telling me I was ungrateful, and annoying.

"Okay," Justin says, his face snapping back into a smile. "If you won't entertain me, I'll do yoga with you. Let's go do some downward dog in the bedroom, huh?"

✂

I know we haven't talked in a long time but I was thinking you should get your BRCA1 and 2 tested. Just because your likelihood is higher. Anyway.

Hope you are doing well.

Leah

P.S. first thing that comes to mind.

Sister.

Sabine Jordan

27 Riverbend Dr. SE

Calgary, AB

T2C 3K9

Printed in Thailand

It's not that I dislike the taste of raisins; rather, I don't understand their purpose. I'm sitting here, pondering why someone would take perfectly good grapes and leave them out in the sun to shrivel, when Justin lets himself in. I left the door unlocked to see whether or not he would knock. Or perhaps because I was pretty sure he wouldn't.

"You ready to go?"

I stir the sogginess of my cereal, not fully awake. "You're early."

"I know; the roads are bad, and if we don't make it to your appointment on time, we won't make it to the theatre on time, and I hate missing previews."

"You're early. I'm not ready."

He kisses the top of my head. "Come on, say it. Say *good morning*. You know you want to."

"Good morning," I say.

"That's my girl. Hey, you know, if you moved back home, I wouldn't be early. I wouldn't be late, either. I would just *be*."

✂

Justin lays on ~~his our~~ his bed while I pack, massaging my prosthetic breast in his left hand like a stress ball. I have booked a ticket on the Greyhound to go to Edmonton for three days to stay with his sister and look for a new home base from which this life can continue. Justin will take my car and meet me up there after he is finished work on Friday, and we will drive home together.

"Need me to sit on your suitcase?" Justin offers. "You know, close it up?"

"It's a three-day trip," I say. "I'm just apartment hunting."

"Pick a good one," he says. "I don't want to live in a hole." And then, when I glare at him, "*What?* Jeez, you have no sense of humour."

"Gimme my boob."

He tosses it at me, underhand. "My sister said to bring your bathing suit. They have that new hot tub in the backyard now."

"I forgot." I turn away from him and walk towards the closet. (89

"I hate it when you walk away from me," he says, half kidding.

"What?" My underwear is all mangled together in the

drawer, the string of my bikini wound around a pink bra.

"You know, ever since you walked off that beach in Penticton. You ruined it for me. I used to love watching you walk away. You know, cuz of the bum. But now ... "

"I didn't walk off the beach," I say. "I just needed a second. You caught up to me, like, two seconds later."

"It was *way* longer than that. You just don't remember because you were the one walking away."

"Do we have to talk about this?"

"Whatever," he says. "We don't. But I'm right."

"No," I say, "I went to the edge of the water. You followed me. I told you to stop following me, and I walked to the car, where you followed me again, and then we drove back to the hotel. How do you not remember that?"

"You never let me get close enough to tell me to stop following you. And it took at least a half an hour before you finally came to the car. And I *wasn't* following you. How do you think all our food and towels got packed up? You came to the car because I did."

"I would never have done that. I was too mad at you." I turn back to the drawer in an attempt to pull my swimsuit free. When I turn back, he looks unusually happy. Unusually happy given the context. Not unusually happy for Justin.

"Well, you're not mad at me anymore," he concedes. "Can I sit on a suitcase now?"

✂

Last time I checked, Sabine was living with a man twice her age in a house in Riverbend, working only when she felt like it, keeping watch over a full garden in their backyard. I had cancer, and she was living with a man twice her age in a house in Riverbend. They were engaged. They weren't engaged. Depended on who you talked to. It wasn't even that long since she'd called off the first wedding.

I tried to picture my meticulous sister pulling weeds, her delicate khaki knees leaving little indentations in the soil bed.

Like everyone else in my life, Cancer told me to ease up on Bean. Or at least, it felt that way. I dreamed about her at night, braiding my hair like she had done once when we were little, braiding my hair and then braiding the braids, until they formed one massive super braid, a maze. I woke up oddly relaxed, and spent the next fifteen minutes trying to recount all the things I hated about her. Her raw ragged fingernails. Her snooty over pronunciation. My mother's consistent preference.

"Oh, go easy on her," my tumour said. "When are you ever going to let that go? You've got a full-time job just dealing with me right now. Pay attention!"

THANK YOU FOR THE
RECOMMENDATION.

Ms. Leah Jordan
2136 Apt. C 22nd St. NW
Calgary, Alberta

T2M 1Z7

I remember house-sitting once, for Justin's boss, a widower who made up for his lack of companionship by purchasing two cockatiels, for which he built a massive cage that he kept in his bedroom. I remember feeling awkward sleeping in someone else's house. This was, of course, before I learned to sleep at the hospital, in an orchestra of voices and coughing and moaning and the whirring and beeping of life-confirming machinery.

Tucked into his boss' sheets, we read simultaneously, our bodies pointed in different directions. Justin, splayed on his side facing the foot of the bed, fiddled with my bare toes. The room, we had discovered earlier, had no light fixture, but rather a massive bay window that lit the room through natural sunlight. The setting sun made it harder and harder to read, the letters squirming in front of my eyes. Justin was bored, his newspaper seemingly less appealing than my novel. Justin reads his newspapers at night, rather than first thing in the morning. He tickled the crevice between my first and second toes.

"Get up here," I say. "Let's just go to sleep."

The room dimmed, and with no light, we fell asleep, my heel in the arch of his foot, our toes touching.

I awoke, semi-conscious, to a high-pitched screeching, and fumbled for our bedside lamp before realizing where we were. Justin rolled over, mumbling, "Lee ... "

"The birds," I said, as it occurred to me. My eyes focused. They were suddenly hushed, staring at me. "Shhh ..." I said. "Maybe they'll stay quiet."

He rolled onto his stomach, not fully awake. The birds and I matched gazes until my eyelids felt heavy.

There, is, however, an unwritten law with birds that states that birds may only squawk if it a) annoys the hell out of someone, or b) involves waking someone up, or c) both.

"I hate you," I informed them.

Justin, assuming I was talking to him, asked, "What?"

We laid beside each other, eyes wide behind closed lids. We fidgeted with the sheets, testing the comfort of different sleeping positions. Finally, he rolled over and ran his hands down my back. I knew what he wanted, but didn't respond. Maybe it was the fact that we were in his boss' house. Maybe it was the birds. They were pecking at each other's faces. It would have been comical, if they didn't look so sadistic.

When he persisted, I asked, "With them watching us?"

"Hey," he countered, "we have to watch them."

"Throw a sheet over their cage," I said.

There was something non-spontaneous about being in

someone else's home, even though that person wasn't home. We crept to the bathroom down the hall and brushed our teeth at the double sink. My side refused to drain. I spit in his.

✕

What the contents of a man's fridge will tell you.

Justin and I haul the heavy bags from the trunk of my father's car. The plastic handles cut into my palms. I ignore Justin's running commentary as we unload and stock the fridge.

"Chocolate flavoured peanut butter? I didn't know they made this! Makes me wish I wasn't allergic to nuts."

EZ-Squeeze Mayonnaise. "Genius, pure genius."

Triple Threat Cold Cuts (ham, salami, pepperoni). "Makes me want a sandwich."

"Dad," I say, "you need protein." Despite his crappy purchases, he has lost weight since I was diagnosed, and I see it more now, how deflated he looks. No longer the stocky, robust dad of my childhood. My inflatable dad, one you could cling to in a pool to stay afloat.

"Cold cuts are protein," he says. "Peanut butter is protein."

"Cold cuts are fat," I say. "If you're going to eat animal carcass, at least eat something that hasn't had all the nutrients stripped out of it."

"Leah never lets me eat meat," Justin pipes up. On our second date, he'd commented on the PETA advertisement I had taped to the fridge, the heartbreaking face of an infant pig.

"Is it wrong," he joked, "that this just makes me hungry?"

✕

During my last checkup, there is a conference going on in one of the hospital auditoriums. I hear laughter as I pass by, my hands wrapped around a cup of coffee, the cardboard barrier protecting my palms from the heat.

"After I had been debulked …" the voice inside is saying, and I slip in and stand with my back against the heavy double doors. The speaker is probably only a few years older than me, both in the traditional sense, as well as in years past remission. I judge this by the length of her hair, a dark curtain falling just an inch above her shoulders. Her lingo is specific to ovarian cancer, but the underlying verbs and adjectives are the same, this cancer dialect I picked up in vivo. She points out warning signs — bloating, frequent urination, nausea, indigestion, constipation, diarrhea, menstrual disorders, pain during intercourse, fatigue, backaches, abdominal and pelvic pain, irregular vaginal bleeding. There are still no reliable tests, she informs us, but there is screening. CA-125. BRCA1 and 2. Transvaginal ultrasound. I should not know what these things are. I clutch my coffee and my doctor's reassuring words.

"If someone gave me the choice," the speaker says, then, and I twist the cardboard sheath around the outside of my cup, "if someone offered me the opportunity to go back to my life before, I wouldn't take it. I am who I am now not *in spite* of my cancer, but *because* of it." The coffee burns my tongue, numbing it against the second sip. "It has taught me how to *live*."

⋉

Sabine was the family liar, but I tried it out a couple of times, too. Bean's lies were always well-formed, elaborate, and fluently executed; she'd perfected the impassive look of someone glancing out from behind a magazine, pretending not to care: "I'm just going to spend the night at Cassandra's; she got a great cookbook for her birthday and we wanted to make tomato quiche." Mine were stunted and impulsive, borderline implausible. We tested our parents, and each other, Bean's scripted deceit and my bumbling falsehoods competing for rewards — a forbidden night past curfew, a diversion of blame, a forged absence from afternoon classes, our parents' alarm, attention.

I remember a few of my failed attempts, the lies my parents never really fell for: "I failed my algebra test." "Is it normal to have red marks all over your stomach?" "I filled the dishwasher with liquid soap and now there are bubbles pouring out of it."

"Mom, okay, give it a break, I was just, you know, kidding? It was a joke. I thought it would be, like, funny or something."

In Sabine's fibs, she was good. In mine, I was bad.

✂

In the Greyhound terminal, my dad orders an egg salad sandwich. He forgets that I don't eat chicken-fetus-salad sandwiches, and offers to buy me one. I settle for a flax bagel. Death-free. In between bites, he tells me about how my mother used to get me to eat seafood. His breath smells of dill. The disproportionate amount of mayonnaise in his sandwich has softened the bread.

"She would take the little shrimp and tell you they would be sad if you didn't eat them, because they wouldn't be fulfilling their shrimpy destiny. And then, once you ate *one*, she'd tell you all the rest would want to be with their friends, and you couldn't leave them behind." He laughed, "She used to make crying noises. You remember?"

"I remember," I say. "Just like Mom, she never accepted that I wanted to be a vegetarian. She was always telling me how wasteful it was. I ate them, but never happily."

"Aw," he says, "poor shrimpies."

"Dad!"

"She knew your weak spot," he points out, and takes his last bite. The bread is so soft I can no longer tell where it becomes egg. The sandwich, even outside of his mouth, looks chewed.

A line from my terminal snakes like a giant L, from the doorway that exits to the bus down to the wall, and then against it. "I should go, Dad," I say.

My place in line winds up being beside a machine that purports to tell my fortune. All I have to do, the instructions insist, is place my hand on it. There are five metal circles where the tips of my fingers are meant to go. My hand hovers over top of it, flat.

Machines can tell you a lot of things. A machine can tell you what's happening in the war in Iraq. A machine can tell you whether your vital signs indicate you're a liar or not. A machine can tell you whether your token has hit the jackpot and you're now a millionaire. And a machine can tell you whether there's an unusual, sickle-shaped mass in your left breast.

"You will have a great trip," my dad says. I didn't know he was still beside me.

"Sorry?" I say.

"That's your fortune," he says. "You're going to have a great trip. You're going to find a great place to live for you and Justin. And I'm going to learn how to make haggis by myself."

⤬

In order to have a fight, both people need to participate. Justin and I do not *fight*, per se. I've heard people say that it's not the act of fighting that makes a couple break up. It's whether they end a fight on a bad note. That is, if one person leaves.

There is one condition that negates that statement. You can stay together forever as long as the other person follows. Even if you shouldn't.

⤬

I go to Amanda's to borrow cardboard boxes, those she and Kenneth used to move out of their apartment and into a real house, a house where they could raise a family. We drag them out of the crawl space and fold them flat in our laps, cross-legged on the basement's cement floor. Amanda turns the baby monitor up, the static crackling in place of our words. We haul the boxes upstairs, tucked under our arms.

"Do you believe in mother's intuition?" Amanda asks, as though she's been thinking about it for awhile. I think about my own mother, of tugging on her pant legs, pulling at her jacket sleeves. Sometimes she spoke to us as though she were a Magic Eight Ball. Yes. Maybe. Ask me later. No. No. No. No. No.

"Sure," I say, "I guess it depends."

"Okay." She sets her stack of boxes down at in the entrance-way to the garage, on top of the washing machine, and reaches into the dryer. "Want tea?" Her arms are filled with miniature garments.

"Sure," I say.

I sip tea while she folds Solie's baby clothes, smoothing static away from fleece sleepers, peeling cotton onesies off a towel whose top has been sewn into the shape of a hood. "Remind me to buy dryer sheets," she says. "But yeah, about the intuition ... ever since Solie was born, I feel like my radar is crazy. I feel ... *psychic* or something. It's not just

knowing whether she needs to be fed or changed. It's like ...
okay, well, you're going to think I'm crazy, but the other day
Kenny came home, and he had this bottle of wine and a rose
and everything, you know, trying to be all romantic, cuz I
haven't really been ... you know, since the baby, and anyway,
I just had this *feeling*, like ... well like, I just knew that if we
... well, that I was going to get pregnant again. I just had this
sense. And I do *not* want to have another kid right now. And
you know, Solie wasn't even really planned, or anything, so
I was just like, there's no way. And so we didn't. It was just
like, *fate* or something." She folds a pint-sized turtleneck and
chuckles, "Our little beatnik."

"It's not really fate, though," I say, "if you changed it. I
mean, some part of you knew you would get pregnant that
night, right? But you didn't. It never came true. So maybe
it's that your intuition was wrong. Maybe you weren't fated to
get pregnant. If you're supposed to get pregnant again, if it's
really meant to happen, then it'll happen, even if you try to
avoid it. If you don't, maybe it's because you were fated to *think*
you were going to get pregnant, so that you actually wouldn't,
and your real fate was *not* getting pregnant."

"You've lost me." She closes nimble fingers around the cuffs
of two downy socks and twists one into the inside of the other,
tosses them into her pile.

"I'm just saying, if it's fate, it's going to happen no matter
what, right? You can't *change* it."

Amanda throws her second ball of socks at me. They bounce
off my prosthetic breast. I don't even feel them when they
make contact. "You're so funny," she says. "Of course you can
change the future. People make decisions about their lives all
the time. Things just don't happen *to* us. We have to *make* them
happen."

"Really," I say, sarcastically. "So did I make my cancer
happen?"

"I didn't mean it like that. Just ... well, like, I didn't intend
to get pregnant the first time. But I chose to keep her. I chose
what to do about it. Like you, you didn't give up. You chose to
fight. The reason you're still alive is because of *you*. Oh! Crap,

I was supposed to throw a load of darks in so they'd be done by the time Ken gets home. I'll be right back."

In her absence, I stare into the anemic fluid of my tea. We'd made it the quick way, from bags instead of leaves. It can tell me nothing. It doesn't matter. I know anyway. When Amanda returns, I say, "By the way, I have a present for you. I just forgot to bring it. I'm going to be in Edmonton this weekend, but I'll have Justin swing by with it, okay?"

Later I slide a tiny shoebox out of the top of my closet and wrap the box's exterior in pink rattle print paper, not allowing myself to look at the baby Nikes inside.

✕

cleav·age klēvij *n.* **1** the hollow between a woman's breasts, especially as revealed by a low neckline. **2** the series of mitotic cell divisions that produces a blastula from a fertilized ovum. **3** any single cell division in such a series. **4** the line formed by a groove between two parts. **5** the state of being split or cleft; a fissure or division.

✕

My sister always smelled like magazines, like the perfumes tucked seductively between the folds of the glossy pages of *Cosmo* and *Teen*. She did the quizzes in red pen. "What Kind of Drink Would You Be?" (Whatever kind of drink she was, it probably had Rohypnol in it). Coming back from getting blood work, I smelled her before I saw her. The Band-Aid holding the cotton ball over where they'd inserted the needle was already coming loose. They'd taken seven vials. It was probably going to bruise. You'd think she would have called before coming. I was getting good at the whole wheelchair maneuvering thing; they let me drive it myself so long as I promised not to stand up. I wondered if the nurses were going to tell her you shouldn't wear perfume or other scented products when visiting the hospital. This was plastered in all of

the elevators: "Many of our staff and patients have allergies."
They told her my room was authorized visitors only and she
could wait until I was back, if she wanted. She left her name
at the nurse's hub and sat down next to a pay phone, flipping
aimlessly through a *Reader's Digest*.

I rolled backwards towards the elevator, thinking I'd get
a muffin. The phlebotomist always insisted I eat after I got
blood drawn. "Otherwise you'll be dizzy."

✂

One day last spring, while Justin was out running errands, the
doorbell rang. Half dozing, I blinked and sucked my breath in,
sure I must have been sliding into another dream. Stripes of
June light, filtered by the venetian blinds, patterned the edge
of the bed.

When the doorbell rang again, I pulled the quilt off our bed
and stumbled towards the front door, my chapped hands slipping on the edges of the blanket. Justin stood on the doorstep,
behind the screen door, with a Santa hat askew on his head.
With the backdrop of velvet grass and buoyant summer wind,
he looked more like a Jester.

"Good King name I can't pro-nounce," he sang, *"on the feast of
some-one."*

"What are you doing?"

He grinned. "No? How 'bout this one? *Oh come let me adore
you, oh come let me adore you, oh come let me adore you-ou* —"

"How 'bout some answers?" I parroted. A toddler across
the street perched motionless and open-mouthed on a
scooter, watching us.

"You didn't have a Christmas, you know, with the whole
chemo and all," Justin explained, simultaneously opening
the door between us and removing his sneakers by stepping
on their back heels. He kicked these off to one side of the
doorway. "It's June twenty-fifth. Jesus' half-birthday. I figure,
no time is better —" the screen door banged closed behind
him, "for a renewed Christmas celebration. Hot chocolate.
Carolling. Stockings. Fooood." He emptied Safeway bags on
the floor in front of us, spewing packaged deli cheeses, a red
pepper, a massive slug of French bread, a cucumber, and a

pair of fluorescent knee-high toe socks. "I know it's kind of last minute," he confesses. "I just had the idea while I was out, because I know you didn't sleep very well last night, and I thought you might need some cheering up. Oh, wait, I left your present in the car." He kisses me, hastily, his lips salty and chapped.

"Okay," I say, dazed.

He bounds out to the car in his bare feet. *"Oh come all ye faith-ful!"*

✕

die dī *v.* **1 intr.** to cease existing, especially by degrees; fade. **2 intr.** to experience an agony or suffering suggestive of that of death. **3 intr.** to become indifferent. **4 intr. informal** to desire something greatly: I would die for …

✕

No one can tell their autobiography until they know where the story of their life begins and ends. I don't remember what I thought the beginning of my story was before I got cancer, or if I thought about what my story was at all. At one point, I thought cancer was the end of my story. In that case, at some point, I missed the beginning. I am not sure if cancer is the beginning, middle, or end. I have no idea about how the story of my life goes, but I'll make it up.

✕

Some part of me knows I shouldn't tell Justin about the reporter who called while we were broken up, wanting to twist our three years of trials into bathetic prose. But I do.

"Isn't that a total breach of privacy?" I challenge him, already regretful of my decision.

He is standing at the stove, his back to me, sliding a spatula under sunny-side-up eggs. Eggs are the one non-vegetarian food he still eats, though I suspect when he's out, he downs the occasional flesh patty. He flips an egg onto his toast and pulls a chair up to me at the table.

"I guess. Sounds like she just wanted to do a nice thing, though." He stabs at the filmy sac protecting the yolk. I watch it hemorrhage onto his plate.

"I told her we couldn't do it because we weren't together at the time. She said she just needed couples."

He takes a bite. "Well, it's not a party until I get there."

"Justin."

He pulls his long legs up onto the chair, tucks his bare feet up under his thighs. His toenails need trimming. "It's not a bad idea. We could have made a lot of money off that."

"I don't think it was for profit."

"We should do it ourselves," he suggests. "Write it ourselves, I mean, or at least sell it ourselves. I bet my sister could write it; she took a few journalism classes in college. She could interview us."

"I can't believe you're eating that," I say. "That's so gross. Even if I *did* like eating animal carcass, I wouldn't eat that."

"Aw, yes you would. So can we do it?"

"Do what?"

"Do the story."

I tear a piece of dry toast off his plate and examine it for traces of yolk.

"I'll think about it," I say, but am counting on his juvenile tendency towards forgetfulness to dissolve the whole issue, my dissatisfaction included.

✕

The gift Justin retrieved from the car that mock Christmas in June day was small but not wrapped, a plastic bag twisted around a box, a cube about half the size of my fist. I didn't want to open it.

He didn't let me open it; rather, he ushered me back into our bedroom and opened it himself. Inside was a small vial of oil, and when he uncapped the top, it released a hot, high scent, like mandarin and ginger.

"It's supposed to be therapeutic," he informed me. "Lay down.

Face down on the bed, I felt his slippery hands slide chastely up the back of my T-shirt. He twisted the heels of his hands into the grooves above my hips, slid his knuckles up and along my spine. When he reached my neck, he gently untied the bandana around my scalp. His fingers slid through the bushy new growths that had sprouted asymmetrically in the months prior, still too short to style. His hands dropped back to my shoulders, and he pressed his thumbs into the hollows just under my ear lobes.

"Justin," I said, and rolled over to face him. "I feel ... *well*." It came out sounding like *whole*.

Justin slipped his hands to my front, placing one over my breast. The other hovered as though cupping a breast he remembered. We looked at each other for a moment, before he broke out into a smile.

"Well, good!" he said, finally, and then, "Thank God for high school sports med!"

✕

Adelaide would have perched on the edge of the bathtub and brushed her daughter's hair while I sipped watered-down apple juice, cross-legged on the closed seat of the toilet. She would have moved out of my father's basement as soon as she could, scrounging together just enough money for a bachelor apartment, where she and her leggy little toddler would share a bed within four feet of the refrigerator, humming them to sleep. She would give me relationship advice, somehow both of us sensing she was more knowledgeable despite her vetoing all members of the opposite sex since her pregnancy.

She wouldn't have liked Justin, and would have balked when I began mentioning him. Would have said his ego was a little too big, would have said he reminded her of one of those dogs going for a drive, hanging hypermanic out the window, drool rolling out of its mouth with the momentum of the car. She would have known better. Maybe if she wasn't just a voice in my head, I wouldn't have ignored her.

)(six

We have been in this bus for approximately forty minutes, on the road for thirty-five. My seatmate's bare feet are tucked up into her lap, raw and bunioned. The big toe on each foot overlaps the second toe, as though years of squeezing into heels has permanently morphed her joints. I think of my father's goofy smile, coaxing me out of a pout, "If you keep that pout on too long, your face will freeze that way." She is on her way to visit her three-year-old granddaughter. She told me this while getting settled, removing her coat and spreading it over the base of the seat, kicking off her boots, adjusting a c-shaped foam pillow around her neck. She wore an oversized and sweat-stained T-shirt with a grinning zebra, its outline warped by the enormity of her bosom and belly. When we boarded the bus, she asked me, "Where are you off to?"

"Edmonton," I said.

"Oh yeah? Good. You know, every time I ride the Greyhound, I always end up next to people who are going to, like, Red Deer, and then they get off and someone else comes on and the only seat open is the one next to mine. And the person always either gets motion sickness, or files their fingernails, or *totally* reeks of cigarettes, cuz they'll of course have had a smoke at the station, they all do. Do you smoke?"

"No."

"Yeah, me neither. It'll kill ya. No cancer for me, thanks. Chocolate?" She unwrapped a partially eaten twelve-inch chocolate rabbit (already minus the feet) and set to gnawing at its crotch.

I thought, Easter was, like, nine months ago, and said, "No thanks."

"Visiting family?" she asks now, adjusting the bulk of her weight around in the seat, licking chocolate body parts off her fingers, putting the armrest into upright to give herself more room.

"No," I say, "I'm going for a job."

"Have one lined up, or trying to find one?"

The second option sounds so much better than my current situation. "Actually, I have some, um, some different options. Quite a few actually. I, uh, I just haven't decided yet."

It sounds genuine, at least to me.

><

We are on our way home from Penticton, no longer a we.

The words we don't say grow and stretch; my impatient fingers twist together. Sometimes, as a little girl, I felt compelled to be destructive without reason. To throw the ring my mother let me borrow off the top floor of the Glenbow Museum down onto the aboriginal exhibits below. To cover my friends' locker handles with Vaseline. To tear the photos of my parents when they were first dating in half and then in quarters.

He doesn't know that I want to slash the pocket off his shirt. Yes, while he is driving. The not doing tingles my spine almost as much as the doing. Like when I used to run past elderly couples holding hands on their evening strolls. I would smile like a good angel jogger, my headphones spilling rap so overtly sexual it could have easily formed the lyrics to backdrop porn music.

The car's speakers spit the steady beat of carefree oldies, like the music doesn't know we have broken up. I look towards the window, away from Justin, at the families passing us, on the way home from their camping trips.

> *These are the good days*
> *I didn't think they'd come back, come back*

> *Your body knows what you don't yet, and your tongue is gonna*
> *tell it to me*

><

The Greyhound wheels churn the warm snow and mud into chocolate slush. I borrow a newspaper while the woman beside me tries to sleep, playing Brainlinks with myself and whatever random, inked words will work.

Family. Tree.
Night. Ingale.
Oil. Well.
And. Rew.
Still. Born.

My nose itches, and I pinch my nostrils closed between the
first finger and thumb of my wool mittens, a bad habit from
childhood. At recess, the snot would freeze onto my mittens,
making me feel guilty about touching the playground equip-
ment. This was before my body became public property.
Before gloved hands hovered bed pans underneath my jutting hips, slid needles into the crooks of my elbows and filled
vials with my angry blood, wiped vomit out of the crevice of
my belly button.

Back. Lash.

><

I didn't know that my mother invited psychics into our home
until a sick day coincided with one of her sessions. I perched
at the top of the stairs and pressed my face between the slats
of the banister. My sinuses ached against the pressure of my
cheeks against the wood. Sweaty with sleep and flu, I had rolled
the sleeves and pants of my pajamas up as far as they would go.

Her visitor was conventionally dressed, in jeans and a dark
blouse, and she set an infant's car seat down on the kitchen
floor beside the table, a thin blanket draped over the opening.
I had never seen this person before, had no idea who she was.
I wanted to see her sleeping baby.

My mother adjusted her chair.

"Okay," the visitor said. "Cards? Numbers? What do you
think?"

"Just some impressions would be fine."

"Okay. I'll just ask you a few questions before we start."

"Of course."

"Full name?"

"Alyssa Nicole Hyde," my mother said effortlessly. I say
effortlessly because I was surprised at how easy a name I'd
never heard before came out of her mouth. I inched my bum
along the carpet for better acoustics.

"Date of birth?"

"June 8, 1958." June 8 was Bean's birthday. My mother's was in September.

"Number of children?"

My mother smiled, shifted her chair again. "One."

"Marital status?"

"Single." She had removed her wedding band.

The visitor lifted my mother's hands and closed her eyes. Their touching hands seemed to make my mother vibrate with excitement.

"Okay. Okay. I'm seeing a man ... he's tall."

"Let me guess," my mother joked, with a charm I didn't know she had, "dark and handsome?"

The visitor opened her eyes and smiled. "Handsome, yes. But he's blond ... and ..." she closed her eyes again, and I watched her foot slide over and jiggle the edge of the car seat. "And he seems to have facial hair. Not a lot. Not like, a full beard. But some. He's slightly younger than you. You may already know him."

I thought of the pictures of my father in childhood, the pale hair Bean and I had inherited. I thought of my father's round, clean-shaven face.

"I'm also seeing a —"

The car seat awoke with a wail that curled up inside it. My mother and her visitor dropped each other's hands. I slid back from the staircase.

"Would you mind if I —" the visitor grasped for the car seat handle.

"Sure, of course. Actually, I'll just run upstairs for a moment."

I pushed myself to a standing position and leapt down the hallway, light on bare feet. The motion made me dizzy. I ducked into the bathroom and flushed the toilet. I heard my mother knock and enter.

"Leah," she said, "I thought you were sleeping."

"My nose kept running," I lied.

"You know what would be a good idea?" she volunteered, gently. "A nice hot bath. The steam will make those snuffles feel better." She reached for the hem of my pajama top and peeled the sweaty cotton away from my skin, leaned over and nudged the faucet. A roar of water filled the room.

"Climb in," she insisted.

I was old enough to realize she was not telling the truth, but not old enough to realize she was testing the psychic, wanting to see if she'd laugh at the fake name and marital status, picture two little girls in bathing suits bruising their tailbones all the way down a staircase waterslide, picture my mother's tall, blond, and hairless husband slipping chips to the dog.

When she went back downstairs, I snuck naked to the door and pressed my ear against it, but the cold air teased my skin and forced me back into the tub. Defeated, I put my whole head under the water.

❁

bos•om boōzəm *n.* **1** a woman's breast or breasts. **2** the chest considered as the place where secret thoughts are kept. **3** the security and closeness likened to being held in a warm familial embrace.

❁

Sabine and I shared a bedroom until I was nine. I remember the way she woke for early morning swim meets, the fuzzy late 80s pop music of her alarm, the way she'd strip naked in the middle of the room and pull her bathing suit up over herself, a second skin. Her suit would still be wet and creased from the previous day. Outside, it was still dark.

Awake, but not fully awake, I would shuffle into my jean shorts and tank tops, having learned the uncomfortable heat that accompanies indoor pools. Because my dad worked shifts, I was often forced to tag along with Mom and Bean, still too young to stay home by myself. Grinding crayons into colouring book pages underneath the bleachers, I ignored my sister and her slick seal body hovering in anticipation at the edge of the pool. As I got older, crayons progressed to markers, and my own body became the canvas, as I rolled back my clothes and surreptitiously inked swirly tattoos onto my upper thighs, around my bellybutton. Body parts my mother wouldn't notice when my shorts and shirts were straightened back into place.

One particular day I slipped away from the bleachers and through the glass door that separated the pool from the girls' change room, needing to pee but not wanting to distract my mother. The floor of the change room was wet, and hairs had collected in the puddles under my sandals. In the handicapped stall, I washed my hands at the personal sink and saw the soap foam bright blue from the marker on my hands. Struck with an idea, I unzipped my backpack and pulled out the purple and red markers. Sliding off my T-shirt, I drew swirls up the length of my torso, interlocking zigzag ladders marching their way from waistband to collar. Satisfied, I put my shirt back on and darted out to the mirror, pivoting in front of it to make sure none of my artwork was visible.

Flitting back towards the swimming pool, I ran head-on into the legs of a tall grown-up man, who backed up and put his hands on my shoulders to steady me. He had a halo of dark hair, receding at the top.

"Who do you belong to?" he'd asked, and I blushed, certain that, for some reason, he could see through my clothes, see the patterns on my skin. "Do you have a brother or sister swimming today?"

"My sister," I informed him. "I have to come because there's nobody at home to watch me."

"You must be pretty tired," he said. "It's pretty early to be awake."

"Are you a dad?" I asked, wondering if his son or daughter was on Sabine's team.

"No," he said. "Sometimes. You look pretty bored; why don't you come with me and I'll get you a treat from the vending machines."

I looked for my mom in the bleachers. She was watching Bean's coach, but seemed to know, abruptly, that I wasn't where she'd last seen me. She stood up and looked around before noticing me, her expression twisting from concern to irritation. She beckoned madly across the length of the pool, her lips forming silently around my name.

"Sorry," I told the stranger, disappointed at being caught, "I have to get back to my mom. Maybe a different day? I'm here all the time."

⊱

Justin and I met in my last and his second last semester of university, in a Children's Literature class, which he quite aptly referred to as Kiddy Litter. I had just had my wisdom teeth out, and my face and neck were still puffy. A rancid piece of food (granola bar?) stuck in one of the incisions worked its way free during the lecture. As we paired off into small groups for discussion, I swallowed it and cringed.

"How much did the tooth fairy bring you?" he asked.

"Sorry?"

"You had your wisdom teeth out, right?"

"Yeah."

"When?"

"Thursday."

"Yeah, they're brutal. Took me like, three weeks before I could eat anything other than porridge. You don't look that bad though."

"Thanks."

He bypasses my sarcasm, unaffected. "So no tooth fairy money? That blows. Those babies should be worth a ton now. You know, with inflation."

He yammered all the way out of class and followed me during my break. "You know what helps? Something really cold. Do you like Slurpees?"

"Yeah," I said.

He grinned. "Let me guess. You're a ... half grape, half cream soda crush."

"Nope. Solid root beer."

He cocked his head, "Intriguing." He rooted in his pocket for quarters. "So, listen, if I buy you one, you have to promise me something."

(109

"What?"

"No drinking from a straw." He grinned, proud of his own cleverness. "Unless you want to start healing from scratch."

✕

I've gotten good at knowing what everyone's secrets are.

The freckled teenager in line in front of me at the post office is trying to convince his thirteen-year-old ex-girlfriend to have an abortion.

The construction worker half in and half out of the sewer across the street is still in therapy: when he was seven, his grandmother beat him with a lamp.

The scrawny twenty-something tapping her foot impatiently at the train accidentally left her balcony door open: when she comes home from work, she'll realize her Shih Tzu fell off, too eager to play outside and not looking where he was going.

Or maybe I've just gotten good at keeping myself warm at night.

✕

The glass of the window beside me is foggy. I blink, thinking there is something on my contact lens, but my view out the window, smears of street lights in the shadows, stays as blurry.

"I hate the Greyhound," my seatmate admits, spontaneously into the dark. Around us, the tiny bulbs above people's seat provide barely enough light to read, to find one's way to the bathroom.

"Me too," I say.

"Although it's not as bad as airplanes."

"Tell me about it!" I raise my eyebrows up in simulated accord. "When they make you wait so long, when they don't tell you you're going to be delayed until you're actually already —"

"On the plane!" she finishes. "That happened to me once flying to Winnipeg. The bathrooms didn't work. Can you imagine? Two hours with no toilet? I don't *think* so!"

I say, "I was delayed two hours on my way to, to Europe."

This seems to interest her. "Oh, really? Where in Europe?"

"Oh, you know, ah, around. All over the place. The whole,

the whole circuit. Some friends and I went backpacking. Did the hostel thing. I really liked the … old architecture."

"Ohhh," she says, leaning up against the window, "I always wanted to go to Europe." Her head hovers precariously close to the faded and backwards letters D I E smudged onto the glass. No one has bothered to wash them off, not even the snowfall.

"I'd love to go again, you know, travel some more," I say, "But my boyfriend has a job here, and, and I can't decide whether or not to marry him and settle down or whether or not there are still things I want to do and see." This sounds like a wishy-washy valedictorian speech, but I keep going, "Whether I want to go back to school, or travel some more, or spend some time volunteering or, you know. But I'd like to be able to have a baby and not put that off forever either. I don't know." Have I said the right thing? This life, this lie, is it believable? I tell her it all depends on money of course, and on my boyfriend, and on my family. I quite possibly overcompensate with, "There's so much I'd like to do, you know, but a lot of it is probably pretty much impossible."

"Oh, don't say that," she chides, adding, "When I was your age …" She stops, and then, "You must be, what, twenty-one, twenty-two? Anyway, I was married at twenty-two. Which was even on the late side, then. We didn't have much money at the time, so we didn't do a big honeymoon, even though I would have loved to go somewhere fancy — well I'd had my heart set on Italy, but anyway. We had just bought a car, though, so we drove it through the mountains together, around Banff and Jasper and Kananaskis Country. I didn't hate long car rides back then as much as I do now. It was nice, though, just being able to escape for a few days, end up wherever you end up. We always said we'd do a road trip again, but then we had our boys and it just didn't happen."

She hasn't yet asked me what I do, I realize, or what my boyfriend is like, or what else I've done in my life, or for that matter, what my name is, and this makes my insides itch with the same restless sensation that accompanies needing to pee. Ahead of me, my brain is writing more answers than I will get to say, more stories than I will get to tell.

✂

It has been said that love is something one can fall both *into* and *out of*. It must be, then, something like a hamster's ball, transparent and spinning, and you're all scrambling and bumping up against each other on the inside. Sometimes the escape is on the top and then two seconds later the escape is beneath you. Sometimes it won't open even if you try. You push your face up against the air holes in the sides of the ball, but even this motion causes the whole thing to upset again.

Love Lessons from Cancer

Calgary Couple Shares Wisdom Learned

Ask Justin Frey what he's learned about relationships and he'll tell you: You have to take them lightly. He says the word lightly while holding up his fingers to symbol quotation marks. "I don't mean that you shouldn't take your relationships seriously," he says, quick to clarify. "You have to do that too. But if you take it too seriously, you'll suck all the fun out of it. And when the going gets tough, if you don't have fun, you won't have anything."

And Frey, 25, a computer programmer, has had his fair share of tough. He first met his soul-mate, Leah Jordan, also 25, in a literature course they were both taking. Jordan was in the process of completing a bachelor's degree from the University of Calgary. The two hit it off, began dating, and before long had moved in together. It was in 2004, however, that this couple's bliss turned to terror. Jordan, then only 24, was diagnosed with breast cancer, had a simple mastectomy, and spent the next several months in and out of hospital, undergoing chemotherapy. Frey recalls his girlfriend, "She had one [breast], was totally bald,

and had lost all her curves ... but I still wanted to spend every second with her."

There were times both Frey and Jordan feared that she would die. It took six months until the cancer went into remission, and Jordan was able to slowly resume her regular life. Part of celebrating included a week-long relaxing vacation to the Okanagan, British Columbia, this past summer.

The couple doesn't know what their future holds, but they know all too well not to take it for granted. "Going through this has made us see everything in a new light," Frey says. "Cancer cemented our relationship — none of those trivial things people worry about matter anymore. The only thing that matters is that we're together."

Currently, the lovebirds, who have learned the true meaning of the phrase "in sickness and in health," are planning to relocate to Edmonton, Alberta, where Jordan plans to pursue an academic career.

Your heaving bosom
Leaping into eager hands
Groping brings much joy

)(the push-up version

Additional Support for Readers

History)

I fold and refold the Okanagan map in my hands, blue river veins.
As a child, I would repeat my own name over and over until it
sounded foreign on my tongue. Maybe it can work backwards too
— if I say ex-boyfriend enough, it will start to sound familiar.

Cleavage emerged from a short story, which was the final
assignment in a creative writing class at the University of
Calgary. Originally, it focused on the road trip taken by Leah
and Justin, and the awkward drive home after having broken
up. While writing *Cleavage*, I'd also just started researching
my psychology undergraduate thesis in psycho-oncology — the
psychology of having and dealing with cancer. I think the pri-
mary goal of a writer is to create and explore complexity, and
an illness certainly intensifies emotions, both negative and
positive; it also creates a lot of reorganization and renegotia-
tion of one's life. Combining a cancer diagnosis at a young age
with an unstable long-term relationship between two incom-
patible twenty-somethings gave me lots to work with; so much
so that, when the short story version of *Cleavage* was handed
in, the feedback I got said it read more like a novel waiting to
happen. The goal of the following year's class (Novel Length
Manuscript) became making it happen.

Fact vs. Fiction)

Once, during a particularly angsty bout of teenagehood, Sabine
stole all the tampons from my purse. This was three and a half days
after the boy I liked performed a song during a school pep rally, a
sort of wah-wah rock 'n' roll song with another girl's name in it. I
went down into the ravine behind our house and sat with my feet in
the stream for a long time, twiddling the sludgy leaves with my toes.
I remember being totally eight-tenths of the way to killing myself.

118)   I've told friends that I've met since writing *Cleavage* that
they're lucky they met me afterwards, because I can guaran-
tee they're not interwoven into the novel in some way. Much

like *Cleavage* is a patchwork quilt of Leah's life and thoughts, the novel has served as a hodge-podge of my own experiences. Those who know me very well can find pieces of my life within the novel: I did live in a shady basement suite (nicknamed the Hobbit Hole for its low ceilings); I did once visit a psychic who forgot my name mid-session; my parents are divorced; I do own a cat; I do ride the c-train facing the opposite direction; I do read the Sun as opposed to the Herald. Those who know me will also likely find pieces of themselves and significant moments, albeit disguised, interwoven within the text. I won't embarrass anyone by saying what parts belong to whom.

At the same time, I made a point to deviate from real-life events in specific ways. While my psycho-oncology research was on ovarian cancer in older adults, I chose breast cancer for Leah and made her young so that her story remained distinct from the narratives in my thesis. Additionally, Leah was a fun character to write in that she and I have a few significant differences, such as her fear of intimacy and her lack of ambition and motivation toward her job. Furthermore, I've never experienced a serious illness. Having cancer gives Leah permission, in a sense, to do and say a lot of things that aren't typically acceptable. Modern society really emphasizes rationality and keeping one's emotions in check, but with Leah, I was able to really explore the dark side of a person's psyche, and the cynical things we all think but don't say aloud.

Cancer)

I am sick of the pink ribbons. Slap a pink ribbon on stationery, stuffed poodles, bracelets, toques, car windshields, lapels. Silly, smiling women walking for a cure, shouting empowerment in the air, clutching their mothers and daughters to their chests. They think the pink ribbons are points — collect enough and breast cancer will disappear. They don't understand. This game has endless levels. You can play as long as you want.

I've referred to *Cleavage* as my anti-thesis because the research I did that year essentially talked about life lessons learned from cancer and how one can triumph over and grow from this diagnosis. However, the women I interviewed also expressed the view that talking about their negative feelings and fears was discouraged, and that the "Pink Culture" of women's cancers focuses more on ribbons and raising money as though this will somehow make all the bad parts of cancer go away. While some individuals may be able to integrate a cancer diagnosis into their lives and make sense of it, having an illness is still a serious, life-changing stressor that, as I've said before, severely complicates one's life. In Leah, I wanted to express the dark side of cancer and the pain it causes (essentially the view that cancer patients often feel they need to hide to protect their family and friends).

Early Drafts / Deleted Scenes)

In its short story version, none of the characters had names except for Leah and characters who had died or were about to die (e.g., Adelaide Kaltenbach, Leah's cat Eightball, the list of the sick at church, etc.), to emphasize Leah's self-identification with death. However, this proved problematic as the story got longer. It gets confusing, for example, in cases of dialogue between two individuals of the same gender (at which point one starts to run out of distinguishing pronouns). *Cleavage* was probably half to three-quarters completed when Leah's friends and family acquired monikers.

At one point, I also experimented with a scene from Justin's perspective, which my editor effectively squelched, as it was too discordant with the rest of the text.

Characters)

Our two-year anniversary falls during the last two weeks that I have two breasts. Justin finds his old clarinet and plays the opening notes to a vaguely familiar song, so sweet and gentle that I cry. He says, "Thank God for high school band."

We eat soft Cheetos under the kitchen table, using sheets as the walls to his makeshift fort. He eats with his left hand and keeps his right on my sacrificial breast. "I'm Cheeto ambidextrous."

Justin was, by far, the most difficult character to write. My classmates, who served as my editors for the year, were ambivalent towards him, depending on the chapters I handed in that week. One week he was "too sweet," and then, when I tried to remedy this, he was "too much of a jerk," and people were starting to ask why Leah was with him in the first place. Interestingly, I think the class' ambivalence towards Justin mirrored how Leah feels about him. He's too charming and cheerful to hate, and yet too annoying and immature to really be that fond of. I can say that my own feelings towards him changed as the book progressed, too.

Questions)

It has been said that love is something one can fall both into and out of. It must be, then, something like a hamster's ball, transparent and spinning, and you're all scrambling and bumping up against each other on the inside. Sometimes the escape is on the top and then two seconds later the escape is beneath you. Sometimes it won't open even if you try. You push your face up against the air holes in the sides of the ball, but even this motion causes the whole thing to upset again.

The question I get asked most often is, "So, are they together in the end?" In the short version, Leah and Justin were not together at the end of the story. However, once I decided *Cleavage* was going to be a novel, I debated back and forth how I myself wanted it to end. The conclusion I came to was that, for these two, the status of their relationship is never that clear-cut, and they are never really on the same page, even when they are living together. With that in mind, there was no way *Cleavage* could end with their relationship either being fully committed or fully over. I think in movies, the couple being together in the end is the desired outcome, while in this case, I'm not sure whether the reader wants Leah and Justin to stay together or not. I'll leave it up to the reader to decide what kind of relationship these two would have six months or a year after the novel ends. It's important to remember that Leah is an unreliable narrator, and that every character in the book has a different view and interpretation of the circumstances. Leah and Justin, in particular, would define the status of their relationship in drastically different ways. Just because one of them says one thing doesn't mean that's really the truth.

)(acknowledg-
ments

Thanks to the Literary Kaleidoscope Book Club for recog-
nizing and supporting *Cleavage* in its early forms, to the
Psychosocial Oncology Department and Tom Baker Cancer
Centre in Calgary, Alberta, for the background knowledge,
the staff at NeWest, and to the University of Calgary English
and Psychology departments.

    I would like to thank those who made significant contri-
butions to this novel, to my education, or to my life (and,
in many cases, all three): Suzette Mayr, Nicole Markotić,
John Siddons, Robyn Read, Jonathan Ball, Freya Nichol,
Luke Devlin, Aly Hasham, Nikki Croft, Caleb Zimmerman,
Ashley Sperling, Katie Hyde, Jennifer Lamborn, Francis
Moon, Shannon Jones, Nicole Petrowski, Maddy Cooper,
Jennifer Lau, Hannah Lee, Eisha Alemao, Brett Kowalchuk,
Cherinne Kilroe, Adriana Chubaty, Nicole Blaszczack, Nicole
van Kampen, Andrea Bures, my parents, my immediate and
extended families, Elena Bischoff, David Gishler, Susan
McDermott, Dave Taylor, my little Taylors, and especially
Alyssa Adair. You all know why.

Theanna Bischoff was born and raised in Calgary, Alberta. Before moving to Toronto to pursue graduate studies in Psychology, she completed a BA Honours Degree in Psychology at the University of Calgary with a Concentration in Creative Writing. Her research has explored how women experience a cancer diagnosis, as well as the development of creative writing skills in adolescents. *Cleavage* is her first novel. For more information, visit www.theannabischoff.com.

The text of this book is set in Filosofia, a typeface designed by the female typographer Zuzana Ličko. It was developed in 1996 as a revival of the 18th century typeface Bodoni.